# With Every HEARTBEAT

# Other titles by Donna Hatch:

## The Rogue Hearts Regency Series:
*The Stranger She Married,* book 1
*The Guise of a Gentleman,* book 2
*A Perfect Secret,* book 3
*The Suspect's Daughter,* book 4

## Anthologies:
Timeless Romance, *Winter Collection* "A Winter's Knight"
Timeless Regency Romance, *Autumn Masquerade* "Unmasking the Duke"
Timeless Regency Romance, *Summer House Party* "A Perfect Match"
*With Every Heartbeat*

## Novellas and Short Stories:
When Ship Bells Ring
Constant Hearts
Emma's Dilemma
The Reluctant Bride
Troubled Hearts

## Christmas Novellas:
A Winter's Knight
A Christmas Reunion
Mistletoe Magic

## Fantasy Novel:
Queen in Exile

## Coming October 2016:
*Courting the Countess*

# Donna Hatch

# With Every HEARTBEAT

## THE RELUCTANT BRIDE
## EMMA'S DILEMMA
## CONSTANT HEARTS

Mirror Lake Press

Cover design by Lisa Messagee
Interior design by Heather Justessen

ISBN-13: 978-1536980110
ISBN-10: 1536980110

# Table of Contents

# THE RELUCTANT BRIDE

England 1815

Abby shifted, bumping first her head and then her knee, and reached two important conclusions. First, the storage compartment of a mail coach was no way to travel. And second, she was a very great fool.

What had she been thinking stowing away? Now she was friendless, cold, and her parents were probably cursing her to high heaven. Moreover, Aunt Millicent might not be pleased to see Abby appear unexpectedly on her doorstep. Aunt Millicent may be even less pleased to learn Abby had defied her father and fled her impending marriage.

At home, this idea of a grand adventure had seemed so exciting, and the perfect solution for avoiding that horrible man to whom her parents had betrothed her as a child. Now she wasn't so sure.

In the crowded compartment, Abby shifted in another failed attempt to ease her aching limbs. Her toes were numb and her stomach growled so loudly she feared it might alert the passengers riding inside the coach.

With every painful, jarring mile, her courage faded. What was worse—running away or facing the terrifying man she was meant to marry? Perhaps she should have stayed and tried harder to find a satisfactory resolution instead of running like a coward. At least as Lady Rosenburg, she'd be fed and warm.

Unless the rumors were true.

A shiver crawled up her spine. What if the first thing he did as her husband was throw her into the dungeon? Or starved her? Or beat her? She tried to wiggle the feeling back into her toes as she imagined all the ways a cruel husband could make her life miserable. No, she was doing the right thing.

The carriage came to a rolling halt. Voices rose and fell, the voices of the driver and the passengers unfortunate enough to secure travel aboard this rattling trap. A posting inn. It had to be. Perhaps here she could make her escape and purchase passage on a different coach, inside this time. Surely she was far enough from home that her movements would not be traced. Hopefully, no one would remember her face if asked.

Breathlessly, she waited until the voices faded, then lifted the hatch. All appeared clear. She pushed the hatch all the way open and climbed out, her stiff limbs protesting as she unfolded them. A long breath of chill air cleared her head.

She stood in the courtyard of a busy inn situated

off a tree-lined highway. Autumn had turned the trees all shades of gold and amber, like finely dressed guards standing at attention along the road. Her churning thoughts quieted as she beheld the magic of nature. After another bracing deep breath, she turned to retrieve her valise, but it was wedged between other bags. She had to tug hard before it finally sprang free. Before she could close the hatch, footsteps neared.

"'Ey there! Wot you think yer a doin'?" A large hand seized her by the elbow and spun her around.

A man with pocked skin and pointed teeth glared at her. She inhaled sharply as alarm washed over her like ice water.

"I'll 'ave no stowaways 'board me coach."

"Please, sir," she gasped, "I'll gladly pay you for passage. Only keep your voice down. I do not wish to be noticed."

He jerked her forward, his fingers digging into her arm. She nearly swooned as his foul breath filled her nostrils. He leered at her. "Well, then, mayhap an arrangement kin be made, eh?"

"What is the fee, sir?" She held her breath, fearing his words.

"You give me all yer money, and yeself for tonight, and we'll see wot we kin do t' keep yer li'l secret." He pulled her in roughly until her body

3

pressed against him and lowered his head toward her mouth.

"No!"

She swung her hand, but before it reached his face, he caught her arm and let out a chilling laugh. Cold fear seized her lungs. He jerked her into his arms, his mouth twisted into a sneer. Fear turned to fury. She would not escape abuse at the hands of a husband only to find it with a stranger!

With all her might, she kicked him in the shin. He let out a roar and threw her to the ground. As she struggled to her feet, she tripped on the hem of her pelisse and fell to her knees. He raised his hand to strike her. With a cry of alarm, she threw her arm over her face, steeling herself for the blow, her heart thudding against her ribs.

"Stop!"

Abby looked up. A finely dressed gentleman strode toward the driver. Another gentleman, not quite so well turned out, followed in his wake, struggling to keep up with the other's long-legged strides. It would have been comical if the situation weren't so dire.

The nearest gentleman raised a fist, his commanding voice ringing out with authority. "What kind of barbarian are you to accost a lady? Leave off at once."

Abby nearly wept with relief. A gallant hero to her rescue. But at what price?

The driver's face twisted in rage. "She's no concern o' yern."

"She is a lady in peril which makes her my concern," the gentleman replied sternly.

"She stowed 'way on me coach and I demand payment." The driver seized her by the wrists, and jerked her toward him.

The gentleman clapped his hand upon the driver's arm. "Unhand her, or suffer the consequences."

The driver shook him off and rounded on him with a sneer and fisted his hands. But before he could make a move or speak, the gentleman leveled a pistol at him.

"For heaven's sake, don't shoot him," gasped the gentleman's companion, a secretary or clerk, judging by his ink-stained fingers.

Her rescuer kept his gaze and his gun trained on the driver. With his other hand, he fished out a coin and flipped it to the driver. "Here. Cool your head in a pint and leave us in peace."

The driver caught it and a greedy light entered his eye as he examined it. Then he crassly bit down on it, a direct insult to the integrity of an obvious gentleman of means.

5

With no outward sign of annoyance, the gentleman added, "And another for your silence regarding the lady and her mode of passage on your coach." He tossed anther coin.

The driver snatched the coin out of the air and turned a sneer upon Abby. "This'll buy me better company than yern, anyway." He turned and touched his cap to the gentleman. "Milor'." He strode away without a backward glance.

As the enormity of her danger hit her, a deep quiver gathered in the pit of her stomach and sprang into her chest. She gasped for breath, her heart hammering, tears burning her eyes. The adventure was, indeed, a very bad idea.

The gentleman knelt beside her and swept off his hat, revealing golden brown hair glinting in the setting sun. His brown eyes filled with concern. "My lady, are you hurt?" His gentle voice contrasted with the harsh tone he'd used with the driver.

"He nearly...I almost...." Her voice cracked and she dissolved into tears.

Still kneeling next to her, he removed his gloves and silently handed her his handkerchief. She struggled to take herself in hand, and, after several shaking breaths, managed to silence her sobs. After wiping her tears with his handkerchief, she looked up into his face.

6

His handsome, smooth-shaven face boasted strong features and a square jaw. A wide, ragged scar ran the length of his left cheek, standing out white against his sun-bronzed skin. But what drew her gaze were his eyes, light brown with gold and green flecks and rimmed with a deep green ring. She wondered if his eyes appeared completely green when he wore similar colored clothing, just as they now echoed the color of his coffee-colored frockcoat.

She searched those fascinating eyes, looking for lust or greed but found only kindness.

"My lady?" he prompted, turning his head slightly as if to shield his scar from her sight.

"No, I've come to no harm," she managed, still lost in his eyes. "Your aid was most timely, sir. I'm in your debt."

"Not at all. I'm unable to resist a damsel in distress." Humor crinkled the corners of his eyes as he extended his hands to help her to her feet.

With her gaze still locked in his, she placed her hands in his outstretched hand. As his fingers closed over hers, he gentled his touch, as if fearing to hurt her. She looked down, amazed at how small her gloved hands looked in his. He pulled her to her feet and stood very near. Her head barely reached his chin and his powerful shoulders looked sturdy enough to carry the weight of the kingdom.

"You're trembling," the gentleman said softly. "May I assist you inside? Perhaps you should eat. I can assure you the food is excellent." He offered an arm and waited, watching her expectantly.

"Thank you." As she placed her hand on his arm, she glanced at his secretary and saw only concern in his expression as well. Abby bent to retrieve her reticule and swayed.

The gentleman placed a hand under her elbow to steady her. "Do you have any other bags?"

"My valise." She indicated the bag lying on the ground next to the carriage.

He made a quick gesture and his companion picked it up. "Forgive me, miss; we have not made the introductions."

Alarm coursed through her veins. She must not be found out! "Y-yes, well this has been a rather unusual day. Two strangers meeting under unconventional circumstances," she laughed nervously, then cringed at the hysterical sound she made. "Let's keep it mysterious and prolong the adventure, shall we?"

One corner of his mouth lifted. "Are you an adventurer?"

"I've always wanted to be. Now is my chance...although it hasn't gone according to plan but then, since it's an adventure; I suppose I should expect a few surprises."

"Indeed."

"So let us continue as friendly strangers, shall we?"

His eye glittered in merriment. "I see your point. We'd better not mar your grand opportunity with such common customs as names."

"Exactly." She glanced up at him, amazed that a fine gentleman would be willing to play along with her little charade. At last she'd met someone not so deeply entrenched with social customs that he couldn't enjoy a little mystery.

"However, I can't exactly call you 'miss' throughout the meal, can I?"

"Well, I suppose you could call me Marie." Her middle name ought not be recognized.

"Marie," he repeated with a smile. "Very mysterious, Marie with no last name. Perhaps I should be equally mysterious—you know, to further your grand adventure filled with mysterious strangers. My friends call me Will."

Grateful she would not be required to give her full name, thus risking discovery, she ignored the breech in etiquette regarding calling a man—a stranger, no less—by his given name. After all, she had already broken a dozen rules of behavior, one more couldn't matter. "Delighted to meet you, Will."

As they entered the inn, the smells of bread and sausage greeted her, and her stomach rumbled in response. Hungry diners feasting upon their dinner filled the main room. No sign of the coachman. A serving girl noisily cleared a table, stacking dishes on a tray, and an innkeeper hurried to them while drying his hands on a towel.

Will led her to an empty table and gestured to the innkeeper. "Bring a plate for the Lady Marie."

"At once, m'lord," replied the innkeeper.

Abby sank into a chair, grateful to be off her unsteady legs and smiled at Will. "Lady Marie?"

"For all I know, you are a visiting foreign princess, but Princess Marie seemed a bit too fantastic so I settled for Lady Marie." His lips curved into a charming smile. As if remembering his secretary, he nodded to the man. "Haws, inform the driver there will be a delay in our departure."

Haws paused, his eyes widening, but quickly regained his composure. "Of course, my lord." Haws set Abby's valise on the floor next to her feet, inclined his head in a brief bow, and withdrew.

Will settled into a seat next to her, close enough that she could touch him if she were to reach out. "Are you certain you're unharmed?"

10

"He didn't hurt me. Only frightened me." She realized she still clutched his handkerchief in her hands. She held it out with a look of apology.

He waved it off. "Keep it."

She dropped it in her lap. With shaking hands, she removed her gloves, frowning at the sullied white kid leather, and pushed back her disheveled hair.

He looked her over carefully, his expression full of sympathy. "You look fatigued."

"And rumpled, no doubt." Truly, she must look a sight.

"Pray tell me; how long were you hiding in that storage compartment?"

A blush warmed her cheeks that this elegant gentleman had caught her in such a childish and scandalous act. What must he think of her?

"Since early this morning. I didn't dare leave when we stopped at the last inn. And now I fear I've been rash. It was foolish of me to travel alone. It seemed wildly romantic at the time." She glanced up to find him watching her with a direct gaze. There was something quiet and melancholy mixed with the kindness in his face. "Thank you for buying the driver's silence. I do not wish to be found."

"Is that why you stowed away?"

"Yes. I have the money, but I was afraid my

movements would be traced if I purchased passage. Someone might have remembered me." She opened her reticule and handed him the equivalent coins which he'd paid the driver. "Please allow me to repay you."

Will held up his hand in refusal. "'Tis all part of the damsel-in-distress service."

"Please. I do not wish to impose upon you more than I already have."

"It would offend my sense of honor were I to take it."

"I'm already deeply in your debt for your aid with the driver. If you hadn't come when you did..." She stopped and concentrated on breathing lest she fall apart again.

Very gently, he asked, "Are you in danger?"

"No, merely...." she toyed with the rejected coins. "I fear you'll think me a terrible coward, but I'm running from an unwanted marriage."

His brows rose. "One that is about to take place, or already has?"

"Oh no! I'd never..." She lowered her lashes as another heated wave washed over her face. "A wedding about to take place."

"I see." He leaned back in his chair. "Is your betrothed so undesirable, then?"

The stark desperation that had driven her from home threatened to overwhelm her. "Terrible. He's much older than I—nearly thirty."

His brows rose and one corner of his lips turned up. "Not so old, I assure you. Yet that must seem old to you when you're only, what?—sixteen? Seventeen?"

"Eighteen. But it gets worse—he's grotesquely deformed. If it were only that, I'd honor my parents' wishes, but he's cruel. They say he beats his servants and keeps those who displease him imprisoned in his dungeon."

His mouth curved in amusement. "Really? How gothic."

"You think I'm making this up?"

"I find it hard to believe anyone could be as bad as all that."

"I realize rumors are not always accurate, which is why I don't believe what they say that every full moon his eyes turn blood-red like the devil or that he grows horns."

"Very sensible of you."

"You're laughing at me."

"No, my lady," he said gravely, but the corners of his eyes crinkled.

A plate of food arrived and she tucked into it. As she ate the savory sausage, potatoes and bread, and drank her hot tea, her spirits rose. Somehow, it would all work out. She would have her adventure and find a way to convince Father to call off the betrothal. Perhaps a season in London...

After a moment Will leaned forward. "So 'tis not his deformity that repulses you most, but his potential to harm you?"

"I admit his face does frighten me a bit, but I cannot bear marriage to a man I should always fear would strike or throw me in his dungeon."

"It would be a terrible waste of space if a dungeon were not used on occasion, don't you think?"

She looked up suddenly, but the sparkle of his eyes revealed his mirth. He wasn't mocking her, he was playing again. The remaining tension coiled in her stomach dissolved. An unbidden smile worked itself to her mouth. "It could be used to store wine. The really cheap kind one serves unwanted guests."

He chuckled. "*Touché.*" With laughter alight in his eyes, his handsome face looked even more striking. Then he sobered and his gaze drifted, unseeing, to the window. Very quietly he asked, "Is he more hideous than I?"

She froze with her fork midway to her mouth. Something so haunting, so sad, entered his voice that a lump rose to her throat. Then it struck her; he was lonely. If he thought himself hideous, it was probably because others had been cruel to him about his scar. She set down her fork and boldly reached out and traced the scar on his cheek, lightly, softly. He flinched but stilled under her touch.

"Am I hurting you, Will?" she whispered.

"No." His eyes fixed on her face and he went utterly still.

"You are not hideous. You're handsome and kind and gentle. Any lady would be fortunate, indeed, to have you."

He stared in disbelief. "You truly don't find me repulsive?"

"Absolutely not. And if I place my hand like this," she cupped his face with her hand, "I cannot see your scar at all. Only your beautiful eyes."

His eyes grew suspiciously shiny. He quickly closed them and placed his hand over hers where it still rested on his cheek. The warm contact sent a thrill of pleasure through her. Yes, she was being terribly, terribly forward, but then, this was a grand adventure with a mysterious gentleman who didn't know her name. Somehow her anonymity emboldened her.

He drew a shuddering breath. "If one as lovely as you can look upon me, and touch me even, then perhaps I am not beyond hope."

At that moment, with his warm skin under her hand and the vulnerability in his voice, she wanted nothing more than to somehow prove he was not beyond hope at all. A golden web of attraction and affection wrapped around them. At that moment, Abby would have given him anything he asked.

The serving girl dropped a glass, shattering the spell enfolding them.

"Forgive me." Abby began to pull away, but his fingers tightened around her hand with an urgent grip as if it were the only barrier between joy and despair.

She held her breath. As a girl, she used to dream that her husband would cherish her, protect her, make her feel safe, and who would need her in return...a man like the gentleman seated next to her. If only it were he that she was meant to marry...

Will released her hand and visibly straightened. "So you have not seen your betrothed when he turns into a demon on a full moon? Red eyes and all?"

She laughed at the image. Something about the way he said it made the idea even more ludicrous than she'd first thought. "In truth, I have never met him."

"Indeed? That's unusual these days."

"We've been betrothed since childhood. A member of my house always marries a member of his. 'Tis been a tradition for many generations. I do not

16

wish to disappoint my parents, but when I learned he got one of his maid servants with child, then beat her and sent her away, not to mention those he imprisons in his dungeon, I knew I couldn't marry him."

A thoughtful frown creased his brow, his hazel eyes turning introspective, his fingers rubbing his lower lip absently. "I wish I could save you from such a thoughtless and violent man. But running from your family is not the correct choice of action."

"I've tried telling my father how much I dread this marriage, but he says I'm too young to know what's best for me. Am I being unreasonable in wanting a husband who will be faithful and treat me with kindness?"

"Certainly not. But you should face your problems, not run away from them."

He was right, of course. She'd reached that conclusion in the carriage. But if she went back, she'd return to the ever-increasing pressure her parents placed upon her to marry that man. And she was running out of time.

"Moreover, you cannot travel alone," he continued. "Where were you bound?"

"To my Great Aunt Millicent. She has always been a sympathetic listener. I'm certain she will take me in. I'm hoping she'll write a letter on my behalf to convince my father to release me from this betrothal. She's the only one to whom he listens."

"How will you get there?"

She glanced at her reticule. "I have been saving all my pin money and can purchase passage on the next public coach that comes through here."

"But you would be traveling in public unchaperoned."

"I know...I couldn't risk taking anyone with me. I didn't know what else to do and I had to act quickly."

He sat up as if coming to a decision. "Where does your aunt reside?"

"She lives in Shropshire."

His forehead creased in a thoughtful frown. "The opposite direction from where I am bound. And a goodly distance, to boot. Still, I see no recourse. I cannot in good conscience allow you to travel such a distance alone. I'll take you myself."

Take her himself? Truly, she'd never met such a gallant gentleman, a knight of old, honor-bound to defend ladies.

"I couldn't impose upon you in that regard, sir."

"Nonsense. I'll send a letter ahead, explaining my delay, and take you to Shropshire in my coach. I'll need to hire a companion to protect your reputation.

I daren't risk your virtue coming under question by traveling alone with me. Perhaps someone nearby would be willing to take the post. I'll make inquiries immediately."

Tears stung her eyes and her heart swelled with tenderness. Was it possible to fall in love with a man she'd just met? He was everything she'd ever imagined in a husband; attentive, a considerate listener, intelligent, possessing of a healthy wit and a mild disregard for the stifling social manners and mores. And that gentleness of soul bespoke the heart of a poet. No doubt he would be a loving husband. And he was clearly a titled lord, so he would be well-connected enough to please Father. Tears trickled down her cheeks.

His jaw tightened and the warmth in his eyes cooled. "You do not wish to travel with me." It wasn't a question.

She blinked. "No, no, that's not it at all. In truth, I was thinking that you are the kindest man I've ever met."

He watched her as if to determine if she were in earnest. Slowly, the hardness faded, replaced by an unbearably soft expression. A moment later, his eyes twinkled. "Don't say that too loud. I have a rather fearsome reputation as well, and I wouldn't wish it to be softened by a mere slip of a girl, even a mysterious adventurer."

She smiled and wiped her tears with his handkerchief she'd left lying in her lap. "Forgive me; I'm not usually such a watering pot."

"A result of your fatigue, no doubt."

She considered traveling with him over the next few days. A most welcome thought. Then her enthusiasm dimmed. Perhaps he was already wed or betrothed. He looked to be approaching thirty; most men were either married or promised by then. Yet, that sadness suggested he had no one to love him. If only she could be the woman who would make him forget his scar, and win more of his wonderful smiles. But he'd done nothing to suggest he had any interest in her beyond a noble desire to protect her. She searched his eyes, looking for clues as to his motives but only got lost in their beauty.

One of his brows lifted. "I seldom meet people who spend more time meeting my gaze than focusing on my scar. And usually they look away because they cannot bear to see it."

"It isn't so bad. And you have fascinating eyes. I can hardly keep from staring at them."

"I pray the young lady to whom I'm betrothed will be as accepting as you are."

Her heart sank as her dream crumbled. "You're betrothed?"

"I was traveling to see her and finalize the arrangements. Yet I dread witnessing her turning away in horror." He turned thoughtful. "If only you and I could both cry off and run away together instead."

She choked. Was he serious? Could it be possible he was developing feelings for her as quickly as hers were forming for him? If only it could be.

He hastened to say, "Forgive me, that was terribly forward of me. Just because I don't make you shudder, doesn't mean you'd ever consider—"

"I most certainly would." Then she blushed. She was taking this bold adventurer role too far. "I mean, if circumstances were different, and if you had the interest—not that I'm suggesting you do—I would not refuse should you express any desire to..."

He grinned broadly and she was grateful she was already seated, otherwise her weakened knees would surely have failed her. His enormous grin transformed him from handsome to positively stunning.

"This will be a most enjoyable trip to Shropshire, Lady Marie."

"Oh, my," she said, a bit winded. "It most certainly will."

"And it shan't end there. All I have to do is show

21

my face to my betrothed, and when she shrieks and cries off, I will go immediately to your father, announce that I've fallen hopelessly in love with you, and demand he consider me."

"Will..."

"I'm most determined. When I want something, or someone, I never allow others to stand in my way."

Weakly, she said, "You've fallen hopelessly in love with me?"

The fierce determination in his expression softened into utmost tenderness. "Do you mind so very much?"

She let out a half laugh, half sob. "Of course not. I believe I'm falling in love with you, as well."

He took her hands into his and kissed them both, one at a time, so slowly and gently that her heart ached.

"Lovely Marie...."

His secretary appeared at his elbow. "Lord Rosenburg, the carriage is ready. Should I have the driver wait or walk the team?"

"Lord Rosenberg?" Abby stared.

Will was the terrible Lord Rosenberg? Her heart stilled.

She looked down at the handkerchief crumpled in her hands and carefully smoothed the fine cloth, tracing the initials monogrammed on the white linen.

"Have him wait. We shan't be but a moment," Will replied.

Abby swallowed hard and studied him. Surely she'd heart wrong. "Y-you're Julian de Malet, Marquis of Rosenberg?"

His eyes widened. "Yes."

She stammered, "you...I...we..."

He straightened and the light of speculation entered his eyes. "You aren't, by chance, Abigail Marie Lansford, daughter of Lord Suttenshire?"

Her heart skipped about a dozen beats and every drop of moisture left her mouth. "Yes."

His lips curved slowly until a grin spread across his entire face. "My betrothed."

She blinked, dazzled by his smile, and thoroughly befuddled by the turn of events. "But you...." Her breath left her. "You...aren't misshapen...or terrifying... or cruel..." she trailed off.

"I am gratified to hear you say that." Again that knee-weakening smile. "You are even lovelier than I'd been led to believe. And better yet, you don't hate the sight of me."

"But you..." She ran her hand over her eyes still grappling with his claim. "You told me your name was Will."

His smile was tender. "I told you my friends call

me Will. 'Tis a nickname based upon my courtesy title of Viscount Wilton. I grew up with that title and only became Lord Rosenburg upon my father's death two years ago. Everyone close to me still occasionally calls me Will."

She blinked. It was all coming too fast. The kind and honorable Will was the cruel and horrible Julian de Malet, Marquis of Rosenberg? Her betrothed? It didn't seem possible.

She squeezed her handkerchief until her hands ached. "The things I've heard about you..."

He took her hand. "I assure you I've never beaten a servant, my dungeon hasn't had an inmate in a hundred years, and I've never dallied with any of my staff, nor have I sired any illegitimate children. I wonder how those rumors got started."

Abby smiled, her heart filling with light. "And you most certainly do not have red eyes."

"No horns, either, not even on a full moon." His eyes danced. "Are you disappointed I'm so ordinary?"

She let out a weak laugh. "Of course not. I'm delighted you're everything I'd hoped to find in a husband."

He squeezed her hands. "Will you marry me, dearest Abigail?"

"It's Abby." She touched his face again. Then

leaned forward and feathered tiny kisses all down his scar. "I will gladly marry you."

He gently traced her cheeks with his fingers and kissed her upturned mouth. His lips were warm and soft, and increasingly possessive.

She would taste those lips every day for the rest of her life. The thought left her bubbling over with happiness. And anxious to return home to marry the man of her dreams.

He pulled her to her feet. "Come, let us return to your home and marry at once."

She wound her arm around his. "What a lovely idea."

They boarded his carriage and drove down the tree-lined road toward their new life together.

The End

# EMMA'S DILEMMA

*a Gothic Vampire Romance*
(or is it?)

# Chapter 1

London, 1816

A bolt of nervous energy shot through Emma as the creature who once was Bennett Ashton glided with the grace of a panther into the crowded ballroom. Darkness clung to him as if the night couldn't release one of its own. Bennett. He was here. With the same horrified fascination one watches a carriage accident, Emma held her breath, unable to tear her gaze away from him. Dear Bennett, her one love, so cruelly snatched from her by the forces of darkness and transformed into a vampire!

Nearby musicians played their instruments with skill and passion. Guests danced, laughed, and flirted. Overhead, cherubs painted on the gilded ceiling flitted through clouds in blissful ignorance. Servants threaded through revelers with trays of champagne. All remained oblivious to Bennett's dark new existence and their own danger. If only Emma could return to such happy ignorance.

## Emma's Dilemma

Wearing a tailored black superfine, the dark, new Bennett slipped between the guests, occasionally murmuring a greeting. Hundreds of candle-lit chandeliers illuminated his midnight hair. His unnaturally pale skin was almost as white as his crisp shirt and cravat.

Emma's heart raced, and his magnetic pull nearly propelled her toward him. She locked her legs and bit her lip. No. She must not give into temptation. He was no longer her Bennett. Regardless of her love for the man he once was, she couldn't fall prey to this monster.

She ran a trembling hand over her ivory silk ball gown. What to do, now?

Standing next to Emma, Millie caught her breath and whispered, "He's here."

"I know." Emma fought back her tears and tugged on the pearls at her throat which seemed to strangle her. "My soul felt his touch the moment he entered the room."

Millie touched her arm, her mouth turned down in sympathy. "You're just like Winifred in *Miss Vernon and the Vampire*."

Emma nodded. She'd identified with Winifred in that gothic novel so many ways. And yet, she'd never dreamed she'd experience the same tragic loss.

If only Emma could return home, throw herself onto her bed, and weep. But she had a decision to make or lives may be lost.

Glaring at Bennett, Millie shook her head, her ostrich feathers shaking. "He has a lot of nerve coming here like he belongs."

Emma made no comment. She still couldn't believe Bennett had become a creature of darkness. Emptiness drove a ragged hole through her heart. He'd betrayed her. The man to whom she'd promised her heart four years ago had turned into something dark and horrible.

When could it have happened? Nothing in his letters suggested he'd changed that dramatically. The early missives he'd sent after he'd arrived on the peninsula had been full of youthful expectation to crush Napoleon's forces. Later, they'd become bleak, filled with horror at the human suffering he'd found on the battlefield. But he'd still remained the same Bennett she'd known, if only a more sober, more disillusioned version of himself.

His letters had abruptly stopped after the one mentioning an illness. Emma's heart turned cold as another thought hit her; the illness could actually have been a transformation from human to monster. After that letter, weeks had gone by without word. She learned from his mother that he'd returned home and was convalescing in the country. Still, he never wrote. How long did it take to turn into a vampire? Had it been painful? She choked at the image of Bennett writhing in agony.

No. She'd remember him as she once knew him; with laughter tugging at his lips, the time they'd thrown more strawberries at each other than they'd eaten, the long walks they'd taken along the seaside, his reckless laughter as he'd finally beaten William Cavanaugh at a steeple chase. And most of all, she'd cherish the joy dancing in his eyes when, underneath a lilac tree with petals falling like snow to nestle in his black hair, they'd vowed to marry when he returned home from the war. He'd been hesitant to accept her vow, concerned that as a girl of fifteen, she might be too young to know her own heart. How noble and honorable he'd been to receive her pledge only on the condition that if her affection had changed, she was free to make another choice. Yes, this was the Bennett she would love and none other. She would live out her life as an old maid, broken-hearted and alone with only her treasured memories.

Millie put an arm around her and gave her a brief, sideways hug. "You aren't alone. I will stand by you, whatever you decide to do."

Dear, dear Millie! No truer friend ever lived. She always mourned with Emma's woes, and rejoiced with her triumphs. Millie never accused Emma of being overly dramatic, or overly imaginative, as others had. Millie remained a steady source of support and love. What would Emma do when Millie married and had a family of her own? Emma would be truly alone, then.

Tears filled Emma's eyes. "Thank you for believing me. No one else thinks vampires are real. I didn't, either, until recently."

"Do you think he'll attack someone tonight?" Millie said from behind her fan.

Chills crawled down Emma's spine at the image of her Bennett sinking his fangs into her neck. What would she feel as they entered her flesh? The initial puncture, the pain, the helplessness as her life drained away...

Shivering, Emma rubbed her upper arms despite the heat of the ballroom. "I'm not certain how often vampires need to feed, but I doubt he'll do it in public. Wouldn't want to get caught, you know."

"No, indeed." Millie fidgeted with the fingers of her long evening gloves.

In a rustle of silk, a third friend joined them. "Who doesn't want to get caught?" Susan's eyes—as blue as her evening gown—sparkled as if delighting in learning some juicy *on dit*.

"Bennett Ashton," Millie said mournfully.

"Bennett Ashton?" Susan's voice conveyed her disbelief. "I doubt very much he does anything scandalous. He's the most perfect gentleman I've ever met. A trifle serious of late, but Papa says he's the most upright man he's ever had the pleasure to know."

Emma's gaze strayed to Bennett. Playing the part of the perfect English gentleman, he bowed over the hostess's hand. As he straightened, he awarded the lady with his blinding smile. Every nearby lady nearly swooned at the sight.

Susan added, "Mama has set her heart on him for me."

"No!" Emma practically screeched. As several heads turned toward her, she ducked her head, her face flaming at her lack of decorum, and used her fan as a shield.

Susan stared before she chuckled. "Oh, that's right. I almost forgot; you have a *tendré* for him, too. Why, half the women under fifty fancy themselves in love with him."

Emma let out her breath and squelched the jealousy that arose at the idea of other ladies throwing themselves at him. No, not jealousy. Only concern that the creature who was once Bennett might make a meal of them.

Shaking her head, Emma softened her voice. "Oh, no, not that. I mean, he's terribly handsome, of course, and very charming, and I admit I felt something for him years ago before he left for the war, but he's not...well..." she looked around and dropped her voice to a whisper. Words she'd sworn she'd never utter tumbled from her mouth. "I no longer deem him a suitable husband."

Millie shook her head vigorously, her ostrich feathers flapping frantically like a bird about to take flight.

Susan's mouth dropped open. "You're both mad. He's one of the most eligible bachelors of the Season."

"Not so eligible, by my accounting," Emma choked.

"What aren't you telling me?" Susan demanded. Her diamond necklace seemed to glare as sharply as her eyes.

Glancing furtively around, Millie whispered, "We can't tell you."

Susan folded her arms. "Well, why ever not?"

Emma gritted her teeth at the superior tone Susan took. At one and twenty, Susan thought she was so much more mature and wise than Emma, but a year's difference between them didn't matter that much. And Susan obviously wasn't in possession of the powers of observation Emma had developed.

Emma fanned herself. "I have my reasons."

"Oh, for goodness sake." Susan said. "Stop whispering behind your fan like a wallflower."

Emma folded said fan with a snap. "Very well, suffice it to say I think he's dangerous."

Susan let out an unladylike snort. "You've been reading too many gothic novels."

Stung, Emma recoiled. Susan never understood her, calling her sensibilities ridiculous. But since Susan clearly didn't possess a stitch of Emma's passionate sensibilities, she'd never understand.

Shoring up her courage, Emma raised her head. "I admit I do have a weakness for gothics, but that's not what I mean. This is serious. No one is safe from him."

Susan's gaze darted from Emma to Millie, her eyes narrowing. "Why?"

Hesitating, Emma held her lower lip between her teeth. If she said anything incriminating about Bennett, she'd be disloyal to the man he once was, the man she held close in her heart. Furthermore, if she voiced her dark suspicion to anyone other than Millie—especially to Susan—she'd be mocked.

36

Emma fingered her pearls with trembling fingers. "You'll have to take my word on this matter."

Susan frowned. "Well, it's clear you've set your cap for him, and you wish to avoid competition, so you're stooping to spreading vague rumors about him."

"Susan!" Emma drew a breath. "That's not it, I vow."

Sobering, Susan eyed her patiently. Then in an uncharacteristically quiet voice said, "You don't believe that rumor about his father's death pointing toward him, do you?"

Emma exchanged glances with Millie, unable to speak. At first, the sudden and unexplained death of his father only days after Bennett's arrival home had seemed an untimely tragedy. But in light of what she now knew...

Millie spoke when Emma couldn't. "That's part of it, but it's truly much, much worse."

"What, then?"

Emma shook her head. "Never mind."

Susan's expression softened. "Please tell me."

If she told Susan, Susan would laugh at Emma. If she withheld her information, and Susan ended up a victim, Emma would never forgive herself. That would be the same as helping a vampire. She would have Susan's death on her shoulders.

# Emma's Dilemma

With a weary sigh, Emma beckoned, and the other two young ladies followed her into an alcove where they could speak without being overheard. "You're not going to believe this, but...I have reason to believe he's a..." she swallowed "...a vampire."

Simply voicing her fears to anyone other than Millie made the whole idea so much more terrifying, more real, more tragic. Bennett was a monster. He killed people. She'd lost him to something worse than death. It would have been better if he'd died at war than to have become this abomination. At least then she could truly mourn him.

"A vampire?" Susan blinked, then burst into laughter.

Millie stared at Susan as if she couldn't fathom why Susan didn't believe them, but Emma wasn't surprised. At first, she couldn't believe it herself. It was all so awful! Still, it stung to have her theory so summarily dismissed. She'd have to take matters into her own hands. Somehow.

Emma folded her arms. "I told you that you wouldn't believe it."

Susan laughed harder, before finally taking control of herself. "Oh, my, thank you. You've always had a flair for the dramatic, Emma, but this is the most diverting tale I've ever heard, even from you."

Emma set her mouth. "It's not a tale."

That set off Susan into fresh laughter. "You cannot be in earnest. Why, vampires only exist in myth. They are not real and I cannot believe even you would believe it." "I didn't at first," Emma said quietly.

Susan wiped tears from her eyes and then let out a gasp as if she'd had an epiphany. "Let me guess; you've read *Miss Vernon and the Vampire* like half the girls in London and now you think you have your very own gothic story."

Emma stiffened, unwilling to admit the novel may have opened her eyes to the possibility of mythical monsters in real life. "I have proof he's a vampire."

Snickering, Susan shook her head. "By all means, tell me your 'proof' at once."

"I will as soon as you stop laughing!" Emma snapped.

This sent Susan off again. Emma tapped her toe, sorely tempted to leave the oh-so-jovial Susan in a room alone with Bennett—it would serve her right. Yet while Susan might be annoying, she was still a friend of sorts, and no one deserved to die by having one's blood sucked out, or become one of the horrifying walking dead.

Never mind that Emma couldn't stand the thought of anyone locked in Bennett's arms, even if he were merely feeding.

Her stomach tightened. Bennett had been an officer in the cavalry, and she'd understood that in battle, he'd been forced to kill enemy soldiers, but that was for king and country. To think of him killing to feed some horrible bloodlust left her alternating between wanting to throw something or fainting on the spot. At the moment, she'd settle for some privacy so she could immerse herself in her pain and have an earth-rending cry. Emma took several deep breaths to hold back her tears. She must not lose control. Not here. Not now.

When Susan finally quieted her mirth, she patted Emma's arm. "Go head and tell me what you've seen."

Emma gathered in her roiling emotions and carefully composed herself. Then, after an encouraging nod from Millie, she began. "When I first saw him after his return home, it was at the Smyth-Buchanan garden party. He was paler than I'd ever seen him. At first I assumed it was because he'd been ill, but now, I know his pallor is because he is one of the walking dead."

"Oh, Emma, that's ridiculous. Any number of explanations—"

"There's more. Then, it was so strange, but he looked at me as if he were about to devour me."

Susan raised a brow and her lips curved upward. "He fancies you, then. He has a grand passion for you."

"I thought so too—I'd actually hoped—but when he greeted me, he kissed the back of my hand and..." she paused dramatically, "his lips were as cold as ice."

Emma swallowed hard to keep her stomach in place. It was all too terrible and she heartily wished she didn't know. But she had to protect herself and others; keeping silent would only put people in danger.

"Your gloves were off?" Susan asked.

"I'd taken them off to eat."

"Oh." Susan look upward, her eyes narrowing as she seemed to remember that day. "Didn't they serve lemon ices at that party? They can certainly make one cold."

"Well, yes, but he would have to have eaten the entire serving bowl to have gotten that cold."

Susan smiled as if she were an adult indulging the fancies of a child, and began fluffing the sleeves of her ball gown. "I'm sure there's an explanation besides his being the walking dead. Furthermore, the garden party was during the day time. Vampires aren't supposed to be able to tolerate sunlight."

41

"Yes, but as you recall, it was a dark and cloudy day, and the rain forced us all indoors; therefore, there was no sunlight to have harmed a vampire."

If the book she'd borrowed from the lending library was correct, according to myth, only the most powerful vampires could walk in the daytime. So, either the myths were flawed, or Bennett was more dangerous than the average vampire. She almost had to admire his unflagging competitive nature. Leave it to Bennett to insist on being the best at everything, even this.

Susan opened her mouth but before she could speak, Millie cut her off. "There's more."

After sending her dearest friend a look of gratitude for her support, Emma moistened her lips. "Mama and I called upon his mother during her 'at home' day. After removing our bonnets, we went to smooth our hair, but couldn't find a mirror. There used to be large gilded one in the foyer, but it was gone. They must have removed it so visitors wouldn't see that he has no reflection."

Susan waved her hand. "Perhaps it got broken. Besides, you don't think his mother is a vampire, too?"

"No," said Millie, "but perhaps she's protecting him."

Emma nodded. If she were agonizing over what

to do about Bennett, his own mother must be positively wretched. Her mother's love had clearly won out. Had enough humanity remained in him that he wouldn't harm his mother? And what about his father? Had he fed on him? That would account for his father's sudden death.

Emma continued. "Two nights past, my parents and I were driving home from a late dinner party, and I saw him entering the graveyard."

His black cloak had billowed as he glided through the swirling fog, as if he weren't quite walking. She'd longed to run to him, to throw her arms around him and vow her heart had remained constant. Yet she'd hung back, fear scraping down her spine as the last pieces of the puzzle snapped into place. He was a vampire. Beautiful and terrible. A killer. A monster.

Emma blinked back tears and gripped her fan as if it alone kept her sane.

Susan shook her head, her forehead creased in confusion. "So? He went to visit someone's grave."

"It was the middle of the night!"

Susan blinked. "Oh. Well, I admit that's unusual, but he did lose his father recently."

"He'd be buried in his parish in the country," Emma reminded her.

Susan's mouth opened and closed. "Well, yes,

but I'm sure there's a reasonable explanation. Perhaps a friend?"

No one spoke. A nearby candle guttered to punctuate the moment.

"And just look at him," Millie said. "Look at the way he moves. No one glides like that when they walk. He's so graceful that his feet hardly seem to touch the ground. And before he left for the war, he wasn't nearly so handsome or charismatic. It's like he underwent some kind of *transformation*." She drew out the last word to emphasize it.

*He'd always been handsome and charismatic,* Emma wanted to say. But Millie was right. She glanced over her shoulder to the main part of the ballroom, scanning for Bennett's familiar form. No less than four women had strategically placed themselves in his path. He moved toward the dance floor with inhuman, predatory grace. One lady dropped a handkerchief just as he passed. He stopped, retrieved the white linen and returned it wearing his signature smile. The lady tittered. Her companions pushed at each other to get in front of the group, clearly hoping to catch his eye. Emma wanted to throw cold water on the lot of them.

Susan raised her hands in surrender. "I admit, that all sounds decidedly odd when you put it like that, but you can't really believe he's a true vampire? I refuse to be that superstitious and I'm surprised you are. This isn't the Dark Ages; we are all educated, enlightened young ladies."

Emma gripped Susan's arm. "I know it sounds mad, but please, please be careful. Court him if your Mama wishes it, but don't go anywhere with him alone. Ever. Not until we can be absolutely sure he's not going to hurt you. Perhaps I am wrong—I hope I am—I truly do. But wait until we're sure. Please."

Of course if she were wrong, she'd scratch Susan's eyes out before she'd let her throw herself at Bennett. But she wasn't wrong. Her fractured heart broke one more time.

Susan's expression softened. "Very well, if it will put your mind at ease, I'll stay away from him. I have no wish to wound your heart by even looking at Mr. Ashton."

With a sudden rush of emotion, tears welled up in Emma's eyes. "You are a good friend, Susan," she choked.

Millie nodded toward the ballroom floor. "We'd best go back before we're missed."

As she stepped out of the alcove, Emma's thoughts churned. Susan hadn't believed her, but at least she'd agreed to steer clear of Bennett. But how could she protect everyone else? She'd never been brave. How could she don the courage that the heroes of her gothic novels always possessed?

A gentleman approached Millie, asking her to dance. With a nod of her ostrich feathers, she gave him her hand and took her place among other dancers forming a line on the dance floor. Emma moved toward the refreshment table and took a glass of lemonade. Sipping her drink, she let her gaze drift idly over the glittering throng. She gasped. Bennett Ashton threaded through the crowed toward her, his gaze burning right through her.

# Chapter 2

Terror shot down Emma's spine. The vampire had spotted her. Seeking aid from any quarter, Emma rushed to the side of a childhood friend and distant cousin, William Cavanaugh, and linked her arm through his.

"William," she said too brightly. "How lovely to see you."

William raised a brow as he turned from the gentleman with whom he'd been conversing. His mouth quirked in amused confusion, and she could just hear him calling her a brazen hussy for approaching a man so boldly, even such an old friend. Then he sobered as he must have spotted the panic in her eyes.

After excusing himself from the gentleman, William took her by the elbow and guided her a little way off.

She glanced back. Bennett Ashton had stopped his approach, and appeared to be admiring a mural on the wall. He glanced her way, his dark gaze colliding with her. Tension rolled off his body in tangible waves. He was waiting for her. To get her alone. To drink her blood and kill her. He must know she'd learned his secret and had decided to silence her.

Or had he merely hoped to use their history to lure her into being alone with him so he could attack her and drink her blood?

"Emma?" William's voice commanded her attention. "Pray, what is it?"

"Oh, nothing," she said with an edge of hysteria to her voice, "I just don't wish to dance with someone, yet I don't dare refuse."

William chuckled. "Not unless you're willing to give up dancing for the entire evening." He gestured to the dance floor. "They're lining up for the next set. Care to stand up with me?"

"Yes!" After another furious glance backward at the creature who stood with his arms folded and a darkly speculative edge to his expression, she lined up with the other dancers and faced William.

"Bennett Ashton is who you're avoiding?" William sounded incredulous.

She nodded once.

"Are you mad? All the other ladies, single or not, are fawning all over him."

"Well they shouldn't be."

"And I thought you and he..."

"No!"

William's eyes narrowed. "What's amiss?"

The musicians struck up a lively country dance. At the last second, Mr. Ashton and some hapless girl who didn't know how dangerous he was fell in line. The hapless girl looked utterly enthralled with Bennett, and Emma gritted her teeth. Bennett's vampire powers had clearly augmented his charm. He wasn't such a society darling before he left for the war.

Of course he was younger then, and not quite so tall or broad of shoulder. And that smoldering look in his eyes was new, as was his new aura of authority. Still, that didn't explain everyone's fascination. If the legends were true, vampires were highly sensual creatures and had almost irresistible allure; it probably helped draw his victims to him so they wouldn't resist when he preyed on them.

As Emma and William worked through the dance sequence, Emma found herself temporarily partnered with Bennett Ashton. Cold sweat trickled down the side of her face.

"Good evening, Miss Hollingsworth," his voice rumbled.

"Good evening," she managed.

## Emma's Dilemma

When had she become Miss Hollingsworth to him? He'd called her his little Emma for so long, even in his letters. She stole a glance at him, avoiding his hypnotic eyes, which, unfortunately, placed her focus on his mouth. She'd almost forgotten the shape of his lips, how well-formed they were, perfectly formed for kissing.

He spun her around, each movement as fluid as water, and then she returned to William. The pattern repeated and she partnered again with Bennett.

"Is there any particular reason why you're avoiding me, Emma?"

There. He said her name. That was much better.

No, not better. The reminder of all she once had and now lost sent a searing pain through her heart.

Wait, did she detect amusement in his voice? Or irritation? She stole another glance at him. His lips curved upward slightly revealing straight, white teeth. No fangs, but perhaps those appeared when he was about to feed, like a snake's venomous fangs.

"I'm not avoiding you," she squeaked, looking anxiously back over her shoulder for William.

They completed the turn and she danced back to William. As she moved on down the line, changing partners and spinning, Bennett's stare pulled at her, and she looked back. Again, his dark gaze fixed on her. Her heart flipped over and she missed a step. She looked up at her current partner as if he were the only person in the room.

"Good evening," she practically shouted.

"Miss Hollingsworth." The man inclined his head, staring curiously at her.

She circled back to William, and they danced their way to the end of the line where they waited until the pattern would draw them in and back up the line again. Breathless from the fast dance, she fanned herself.

William leaned closer. "Has he offended you in some way?"

She snapped her gaze to him. "Who?"

"Ashton. You act as if you expect him to draw a sword and start killing people."

She tried to laugh lightly but it came out sounding hysterical. "No, of course not. And no, he hasn't offended me. We've barely spoken. In fact, I hardly know him. He's very different now than he was before he left."

"Not so different. Just more sober. Are you sure he hasn't done something to offend you?"

"No, no." But she'd have to explain her odd behavior. "To tell you the truth, he strikes me as odd and a bit dangerous now."

51

William chuckled. "Yes, well, we men rather fancy ourselves as dangerous to women. Although 'odd' isn't exactly a glowing compliment."

The dance sequence drew them back into the dance and they had no further opportunity to converse. As she progressed up the line, she partnered with Bennett once again. Averting her gaze from his face, she focused on the dance steps and tried to appear calm. Acting strangely would only arouse his suspicions that she knew his secret.

"I don't recall you being so reticent, Miss Hollingsworth." His voice slipped over her skin like a caress, fraying her nerves.

Unable to resist, she looked up at him. Her mouth turned to dust. He'd grown devastatingly handsome. His cheekbones and jaw had filled out. The spots that once plagued him as a youth had smoothed over, leaving flawless, creamy skin. She gulped. Not merely creamy—deathly white.

As if he never went out into the sun because it burned him.

As if he were one of the undead.

Her heart thudded against her chest so wildly she wondered if all the dancers could hear it above the din of the ball. Smoothly, he led her through the steps. Since they both wore gloves, she couldn't determine if his hands were still ice cold, but in light of all the evidence shouting at her, she had little doubt. He was a vampire. And for some reason, he appeared to be interested in her. Had he forgotten what they once meant to each other and had chosen her as his next victim? Or did he plan to make her his eternal, evil mate?

And why didn't the thought of him drawing her into his arms, whispering into her ear, and then biting her neck, terrify her the way it should? She certainly didn't want to die. Nor could she bear to become one of the walking dead, attacking people and drinking their blood. The thought sent shivers of revulsion down her spine. Why was she so drawn to him with all she knew about him? Perhaps it was part of his vampire powers of seduction.

Well, she'd just have to resist him. Somehow.

Thankfully, the dance pattern led her down the line to other partners, weaving in and out with them, always returning to partner with William. She glanced at her old friend. Perhaps she should confide in him. He'd laugh at first, but he'd listen fairly. And he'd know what to do.

The dance set ended. As William led her off the dance floor, he took her directly to the refreshment table and handed her a glass of lemonade.

"Good exercise that," William quipped.

After taking a drink of the cool lemonade, she snapped open her fan and used it to stir the air. "Yes, indeed. It's warm in here."

He nodded his head out toward the terrace doors, open to let in the cool night air. "Shall we catch our breath out there?"

Smiling, she took his arm. "Why, William, you wouldn't be trying to lure me into a dark garden now, would you?"

"Of course I am. We dangerous males all have such plots in our arsenal. All part of the Byronic image, you know."

She laughed. "Aren't you supposed to be plotting against someone you don't view as a little sister?"

"I daren't risk some father demanding I marry a girl just because I kissed her."

"Oh, gracious no. That might be just too gallant."

Sobering, he raised a brow. "So, what's this with Ashton?"

"I..." she looked away, unable to tell William.

He guided her through the crowd toward the open terrace doors. "You'd best be upfront with him, then, because he has his sights set on you."

Because he still cared, even now? Or because he suspected she knew his secret and had decided to silence her?

She dodged a man who stepped back as he laughed with a group of men. "He's been gone a long time. I doubt he truly feels anything for me any longer. Four years is a long time. His letters were very proper; we never discussed our feelings."

"When he first arrived in London, he made a point of asking if you and I had any kind of understanding, and he made it quite clear he expected me to be the gentleman and step aside for him if we did."

That drew her stare. "He expected you to step aside for him?"

"Most emphatically."

She tried to smile at the thought forming an attachment with William, but her heart ached each time she considered what might have been with Bennett. Why would he go through such an elaborate ruse to warn off William?

She looked up at him. "Did you assure him that your relationship with me is the same comfortable friendship it's always been?"

"I tried to but he didn't believe me. I did vow I wouldn't interfere in any way with his pursuit of you."

She chuckled. "I'm sure that was a vow easily made."

William made no reply. Instead, he turned pensive.

Just before they reached the open doorway, one of his friends called out, "I say, Cavanaugh, I wonder if I might have a word with you?"

William glanced back at her but she waved him off. "Go on."

Seeking the cool night air, Emma moved across the terrace toward the gardens illuminated by moonlight and Chinese lanterns. Careful to stay in the patch of light cast by the open doors so she wouldn't be out of sight and give cause for scandal, she drew in a deep breath. The breeze slipped over her hot skin, cooling her. A night bird trilled and a bird or bat flapped overhead. The stars shone in glorious splendor overhead.

If only she could be blissfully ignorant about Bennett. Discovering that he'd transformed into a creature of pure evil made her want to throw something. Knowing the truth was safer, of course; she could now take steps to avoid becoming a victim, but the truth had shattered all her dreams.

She looked up at the sound of flapping wings. A patch of darkness blotted out the stars, and she ducked slightly as a bat sailed toward her from deeper in the garden, swooped overhead, and flitted off to the right. There were times when she wished she could soar out into the night like that, unfettered by so many social rules. After casting a guilty glace over her shoulder at the ballroom, she stepped out of the light and into the night. A fountain murmured nearby. She sauntered to it, inhaling the scent of jasmine. Moonlight glimmered in the surface of the pool below the water sculpture.

A breeze whispered, stirring the trees. She should have thought to bring a shawl. As lovely as it was out in the garden, she'd better return to the ballroom or she'd catch a chill. Besides, it wouldn't do to disappear and set tongues wagging; people might think she was on some sort of illicit rendezvous, and she daren't risk ruin. Of course, if she died a spinster, that wouldn't really matter, but she couldn't dishonor her family name.

The bat flapped overhead again, and wheeled away, disappearing behind a large shrub. A dark form stepped out of the same shrub. Her breath caught and she jumped as a tall man approached.

Bennett Ashton.

Coming out from behind the very bush where the bat had disappeared.

# Chapter 3

Emma's heart leaped into her throat and she let out a strangled scream. She turned and ran. In a haze of panic, she stumbled and went down hard. Pain flared in her ankle and left side.

"Emma?" Bennett's hypnotic voice slipped over her senses, carrying all his dark powers of seduction.

He would not make her his next victim!

Scrambling to her feet, she plunged forward but pain stabbed her ankle and she collapsed. Frantic, she glanced over her shoulder. He was coming for her. Helpless, a sob escaped her throat.

"Are you hurt?" He sounded concerned, not predatory.

She gathered her courage. Perhaps he wouldn't kill her with the party only a few steps away. Surely he wouldn't.

She tried to speak but her voice caught.

Bennett knelt next to her. "Are you injured?"

He reached for her but she shrank from him and scrambled backward. Her words tripped over each other as she babbled the first thing that came into her head. "No, no, I'm just...er...I tripped. I'm perfectly well. My friends are waiting for me. They'll miss me if I don't return soon. In fact, they must already be looking for me now. They'll probably be here at any moment. And my parents. I told them I'd only be a moment."

Bennett blinked at her frantic monologue and one dark brow rose. "Very well, then we'd best get you back inside." He held out a gloved hand. It shone pale and cold in the moonlight.

She leaned away, loath to touch a vampire, even one as handsome as Bennett Ashton. "I'm fine; just twisted my foot a bit." Ignoring the hand, she scooted backward to the edge of a decorative boulder and used it to help her to her feet.

"Why are you being so stubborn? Let me help you." Without warning, he swooped in and scooped her up into his arms.

She let out terrified yelp and froze.

He made a growl of frustration. "What the deuce is the matter with you? You act as if I'm going to ravage you. Have a little faith in me."

She sucked in her breath at the uncharacteristic sharpness in his tone. "I'm sorry....I just...you're so different now."

### Emma's Dilemma

"Yes, well, war has a way of doing that to people," he said grimly.

*War, and what else?* she wanted to ask, but couldn't form the words.

Shivering, either from the cold night air or fear of being so close to a vampire, she clamped her mouth shut as he set her down on a nearby stone bench.

He knelt in front of her. "Let me see your ankle. Which one is it?"

"That's not necessary. I'll just hop back. I really must return before someone misses me."

"Emma." Bennett leaned in and braced a hand on the bench on either side of her knees. "You are not hopping back."

The sheer animal magnetism of this man she once knew nearly overwhelmed her senses. Her breath caught and her heart thumped in her ears. His black, unreadable gaze drilled into her eyes with such intensity that her mind emptied of all coherent thought except how badly she wanted his arms around her again. In the silvery light, his face took on a mystical beauty. His lips parted, and for a wild, heart-racing instant, she hoped he'd kiss her.

He whispered, "I've missed you." He leaned in and raised his hand slowly toward her cheek.

The touch of death.

60

She let out a gasp and jerked back. "N-no!"

He stilled, lowered his hand. "Forgive me."

Tears sprang to her eyes and she tried to blink them away. How much she'd missed him. How long she'd prayed for his safe return. But now that he'd returned, more mysterious and more handsome than ever, he was something evil.

"Are you in pain?" he whispered.

A sob built up in her throat, closing off her breath. "Yes," she managed hoarsely. But not the way he supposed. Her heart tore slowly, agonizingly, in two.

He gestured to her feet. "Which ankle?"

After casting a longing look toward the open ballroom doors, she raised her injured foot. She held her breath as he gently probed her ankle, his touch feather-light, and more gloriously sensual than she'd ever imagined despite his cold fingers.

"It's swelling," he said. "Of course, I'm no surgeon, but I've seen my fair share of field injuries, and this doesn't feel broken."

Her teeth began to chatter.

"Here, you must be cold. Take my coat."

She leaned away from him. "No, no, don't bother. Really, thank you."

He eyed her quietly. "I can't very well carry you

into the *soiree*. That would scandalize all of London. Shall I fetch your mother and have the carriage made ready? I could carry you through the garden gate to the street."

"Perhaps I could just limp inside."

He blew out his breath slowly. "You are as stubborn as ever. Very well; can you stand?"

A part of her wondered why he was helping her instead of making a meal of her. Not hungry? Too concerned he'd be implicated in her death?

Or did he truly still have feelings for her which prevented him from harming her? Perhaps he wanted her but held back because he loved her too much to hurt her. The thought left her in a state of confused excitement. She must have truly lost her wits.

Bracing her feet, she tentatively stood. Pain shot up her ankle, but she tried not to wince. She took a step forward and collapsed the instant she put her weight on the injured foot. He leaped to her side, catching her, and slid an arm around her.

She turned and looked up at him. His eyes were shadowed and unreadable. He smelled of cedar and something earthy. She leaned closer and drew in another breath of him.

A slow smile formed on his lips. "I can't tell you how often I've dreamed of this."

She froze. "I thought you weren't going to take liberties." She winced at the sharpness of her tone. After all, he had been nothing but gallant.

His smile vanished. He led her back to the bench and saw her settled on it. "I'm reluctant to leave you alone out here, but we need to summon a carriage."

She nodded, her heart melting. Remembering the man he once was, and seemed to still be, she gave him a soft smile and said gently, "I'm sure I'm in no danger here."

No danger as long as he didn't try to sink his teeth into her neck, which, oddly, he didn't seem to be considering. Nothing about him suggested any ominous intentions. Could it be possible she was wrong about him?

A couple strolled by, arm and arm, their voices low, without even glancing at Bennett or Emma.

He let out his breath slowly. "Very, well. I'll return shortly. Please take my coat to stay warm."

She smiled sadly, and shook her head. "You can't go back without it. That would look suspicious. Please just hurry back with my parents."

He nodded and strode away silently. With his departure came sharp reality. All her wishes would not change the truth. He was a vampire. Whatever doubt she might have had about the creature he'd become was now gone. The bat had resolved that. She'd well and truly lost him—not to war or even disease, but to something so much worse. The loss drilled a hole through her so large she knew she'd never be whole. Engulfed in sorrow, she covered her face in her hands and wept hot, bitter tears.

After a moment, she took herself in hand and dried her tears. She couldn't mourn what might have been. She had to think clearly. What to do now? She couldn't very well lure him off alone and try to drive a stake through his heart. She flinched at the image of hurting him. No, she could never do that. Nor could she, in good conscience, let him roam free, feeding off of people, especially those she knew and loved. Confronting him and demanding he leave would only shift the problem to another place where he could harm other people. No, he must be stopped. Somehow.

If only there were a way to stop him without killing him. But then, if he were the undead, he wouldn't actually be killed. Would he?

It was enough to give her a headache. She pressed a hand to her head. But all she could think of was the way he'd carried her to the bench and the gentleness of his hands.

She let out a low moan. Footsteps neared and she lowered her hand, trying to appear composed.

"Emma?" Her mother's voice drifted to her.

"I'm here, Mama."

Both her parents arrived. "Mr. Ashton said you'd twisted your ankle," Mama said.

Papa added, "We'll talk later about what you were doing in the garden alone with him."

"I wasn't *with* him, Papa. He came upon me after I tripped and hurt my ankle."

"Uh-huh." His tone clearly revealed his disbelief.

Mama wrapped a shawl around Emma. "It's freezing out here. I've never seen such a cold spring. Why, it's almost summer and it feels like February. We've sent for the carriage, dear, to take you home."

"May I help?" Bennett's velvety tones wrapped around her with more warmth than the shawl. If only his touch were as warm.

"We've already sent for the carriage," Papa said curtly.

Without showing any signs he'd taken offence, Bennett pointed deeper into the garden. "There's a garden gate back that way which leads to the street. We could help her out there so we wouldn't have to go back through the drawing room."

Papa nodded. "I'm familiar with it."

Bennett stepped back as Mama and Papa put their arms around either side of Emma and helped her to a stand. She sucked in her breath as she stepped on her sore ankle.

"Lean on me more," Papa said.

Emma tried to obey, but he staggered under her weight, his poor health leaving him weakened. She limped, trying to hop onto her good foot and sparing her injury, but every motion shot pain knifing through her leg.

"This isn't working," she moaned.

"Sir," Bennett's voice came from out of the darkness. "If you'll permit me, I could carry her to your coach. It would be faster and less difficult for all."

Papa hesitated as if giving the matter some thought.

"Papa," Emma said gently. "With you and Mama both here, I doubt anyone would raise any brows even if we are seen."

"Very well." Papa stepped back and gestured to Bennett.

Bennett stepped in close and Emma's heart raced but this time, not in fear. He scooped her up and easily carried her toward the garden gate. A laughable feeling of safely enveloped her. Really, she shouldn't enjoy being in his arms so much. She was such an idiot!

Bennett stepped aside for Papa to open the gate before he carried Emma through. Emma rested her head against his shoulder. This may be their last touch ever; she may as well enjoy it. Their coach waited only a few steps away, the horses stamping in the cold. Bennett braced one foot inside the carriage and set her into a seat. Instead of stepping back to allow her parents in, he snatched a carriage robe and tucked it firmly around her.

In a low voice, he said, "I'm not sure why you're so intent on avoiding me, but I really wish to see you. May I call on you tomorrow?"

She hesitated, wanting nothing better than to see the Bennett Ashton she knew and loved. Her resistance crumbled and she nodded, a smile pulling at her mouth. "Our 'at home' hours are from one o'clock until three."

He nodded. "I remember. Until tomorrow, then."

Bennett had no way of knowing if it would be sunny or cloudy tomorrow. He must have become one of those powerful vampires who could tolerate sunlight briefly. Or was he merely counting on the constantly cold and overcast weather they'd had lately?

She nodded. "I look forward to it."

He stepped back. She couldn't tear her gaze away from him. He stood, so confident, regal even, and yet with the faintest desperation in his expression.

After Papa handed Mama in and helped her settle into the seat next to Emma, he turned to Bennett. "Thank you for your assistance and your discretion, Mr. Ashton."

"Sir, I know it looks bad, but I vow I haven't touched your daughter, nor did I lure her out to the garden. I simply came upon her when I was out getting some air."

Papa grunted a reply and got in. As the carriage rolled forward, Emma craned her neck out the window to keep Bennett in sight. He stood watching the carriage leave. She tore her gaze away and leaned back against the seats.

A few moments with Bennett had reawakened all those old feelings, all those old dreams. True, she'd been a girl of fifteen then, but her feelings had been so adult, so lasting, so real. And they were all still there inside her, stronger than ever before.

She let out a breathy sigh. What on earth would she do now?

Heaven help her. She was in love with a vampire.

# *Chapter 4*

Bennett arrived at promptly in their family house in Mayfair at one o'clock in the afternoon. Mesmerized, Emma remained rooted to the cushions of her settee as he strode into the parlor. He swept off his hat, revealing his shining black hair, and removed a pair of spectacles that had been darkened as if he'd held them over a fire and gotten them sooty. He glanced about the room before his gaze landed on her, sending her nerves into a tingling frenzy.

Her mouth dried. Good thing she was already sitting or surely her knees would weaken. How was it possible he was even more handsome than last night?

It didn't matter. She wouldn't let him hurt her or turn her into an evil being.

Although, the though of spending eternity with him...

No. She mustn't think of that.

Bennett greeted Mama, affecting a courtly bow, and exchanged a few pleasantries with her and some of the other guests. A moment later, he made his way to Emma. He took a seat next to her on the settee and looked at her as if she were the only person in the room. "How's the ankle?"

His nearness emptied her mind of all coherent thought. "My ankle?" she repeated.

He gestured to her feet resting on a footstool. "The one you twisted last night?"

She let out a weak laugh. "Oh, that ankle. Still sore, I'm afraid."

He nodded. "I'd planned to invite you to go riding with me, but it looks as though we'll need to wait until your ankle heals."

"Riding?"

In the daytime? How much sunlight could he take? Even with his darkened glasses, surely not much. Just how powerful was he? Or perhaps the belief that sunlight burned a vampire's skin was false.

His dark gaze penetrated her eyes straight into her soul. "You wouldn't mind being seen with me, would you?"

"Seen with you?"

He smiled. "Any particular reason why you're repeating everything I ask you?"

"Ah..." No, no particular reason, except she was so confused. She loved and trusted the old Bennett. And she loved this new dark Bennett. But could she give him her trust?

She drew a breath and took herself in hand. "Forgive me. My injured ankle appears to have had some effect on my wit. No, of course I don't mind being seen with you. I would love to go riding with you when I'm able." Perhaps if she went riding with him, she could decide what must be done.

Bennett listened, watching her intently, as if he would rather do nothing else. She'd always loved that about him.

"We could ride by carriage instead of horseback," he said. "I have a new team I'd like to show you. I assume you're still horse-mad?"

She smiled and tossed her head saucily. "I am, and my father still refuses to take me to Tattersalls."

He frowned. "Certainly not. No place for a lady."

"He allows me to go with him from time to time when he attends auctions in Ireland."

"I suppose that can be overlooked, even by a sophisticated gentleman as I." A self-deprecating smile touched his mouth.

"How fortunate for me," she said dryly.

They shared a smile, and for a moment, all thoughts of his being a vampire evaporated in his sheer masculine presence. Her heart thudded erratically and she couldn't drag her gaze off his mouth. She'd shared stolen kisses with other men, but

71

never him—not even when she'd pledged herself to him. What would it be like to kiss Bennett? Would he be smooth as silk? Forceful, even rough? Or would he be infinitely gentle?

"Are you well, Em?"

"Hmmm?"

"You look a little flushed."

"Ah..." She cleared her throat and finally managed to put her attention back onto his eyes. They were still as dark as onyx, even more mysterious than ever. She swallowed. "I'm too close to the fire. Mama is convinced if I leave the hearth, I'll catch a chill."

A black brow rose. "She equates a twisted ankle with an illness?"

She smiled. "Apparently so."

"A pity. That may complicate our plans to go for a drive." And in an exaggeratedly serious tone, he said, "Do you think she'll allow you to leave the house so sorely stricken?"

She chuckled. "It has been an uncommonly cold Spring. However, if you ply your charm on her, I think she may relent and allow me out."

He placed his hand over his heart. "I promise to keep you well bundled so you don't catch a chill."

In the same overly grave tone, she replied, "You are most chivalrous, sir."

He was chivalrous, and concerned, and gentle—everything that she loved about him before was still there. Was it possible to for him to be a vampire and yet be the same man? Nothing about him seemed ruthless or evil.

"You're very far away," he said softly.

She looked up at him, longing to trace the contours of his face. "I have much on my mind."

"Tell me."

She couldn't very well discuss his secret. What to say? She seized the first thought that came to her. "You mentioned an illness. I assume you are feeling better?"

"I am. It was a long recovery, but I am much better."

Why better? Did he enjoy his new existence? A million other questions flooded her mind, but nothing she could voice. His gaze remained fixed on her in his usual intense way. She moistened her lips. "Er...it's been a long time since we've conversed in person."

"It has. Too long."

"Your letters were few and far apart."

Sorrow darkened his eyes. "I wish I could have written more often. But yours were a welcome contact with home. With you."

73

She examined her fingers. "I had to keep my letters fairly impersonal because my father had only given me permission to write to you if I kept to safe topics such as local happenings and *on dits*."

"I know. It would have been inappropriate to do otherwise. I couldn't tell you how much your letters meant to me, or that I hoped you'd still be here when I got back."

"There was never any danger of me not being here when you got back." She had to look away lest he see the tears in her eyes. She was here, but Bennett—the real Bennett—hadn't returned. Would never return "You are different." She snuck a glance at him to judge his reaction.

He froze, those black eyes searching hers. "Am I?"

Losing courage, she stuck to a safe explanation. "I wondered if you'd return home from the war a bit rough, but if anything, you're more refined, more...confident."

A haunted expression flitted across his face and settled into his eyes. She sucked in her breath at the apparent agonizing turmoil trapped inside him.

He looked away. "I am different. I saw things—*did* things—in battle that I'd never dreamed I'd do. I doubt you'd view any of them as refining. Last week was the first time I'd stepped foot in a drawing room in four years."

She touched his sleeve, aching to soothe his pain, and whispered, "I'm so sorry, Bennett."

He glanced away and shielded his hurt. "Yes, well, I didn't come here to cry on your shoulder."

She withdrew her hand, feeling decidedly shut out. "We've known each other a long time. You can be honest with me. You can tell me anything."

His mouth twisted into a humorless smile. "You're very kind, but I wouldn't burden you with my woes."

"It's what a friend would do."

He gaze fixed hard upon her. "Are we friends, Em?"

Could she be friends with a vampire? She must at least pretend to be until she decided what to do with her knowledge. "Certainly we are."

"Only friends? Nothing else?"

She clasped her hands so tightly that they started to hurt. Was he asking her permission to court her? Did she dare? He watched her with such dreadful hope that her resistance dissolved. "I haven't placed a limit on our relationship, or its potential."

Warmth seeped into his expression until he grinned. "That's what I hoped to hear." He paused. "I hear you received two marriage proposals."

She nodded slowly. "Neither of them were from you."

There. She's said it. His would be the next move. Then perhaps she would know what to do.

"You give me hope." He smiled, promise shining in his eyes. He leaned forward as if to say more. Instead, he glanced at her mother. With a wry smile twisting his mouth, he looked at his pocket watch. "If I'm to impress your mother, I must be careful not to overstay my visit, lest she think me uncouth." He stood and offered a brief, proper bow. "And now, with your permission, I shall endeavor to convince your protective mama to allow you to have an outing with me tomorrow."

She returned his smile, nearly speechless at the beauty of it. "Please do."

"Till tomorrow then."

"I look forward to it."

He awarded her another lovely smile and turned to seek out Mama. They shared a brief conversation, with Mama only looking Emma's way three times. Finally, Mama's shoulders relaxed and she nodded, smiling. Bennett strode to the door. At the doorway, he turned, gave her another blinding smile, and left.

Emma leaned back against the cushions, smiling dreamily, her head filled with visions of Bennett's handsome face, his winning smile, the sign that he needed her to shine light into those dark places left by war and hardship. She couldn't wait until tomorrow.

A form crossed in front of her line of sight and someone plopped down in the cushions next to her.

William leaned in. "I take it you've overcome whatever aversion you had for Bennett Ashton?"

"Hmmm?" As she focused on William's face, clarity rushed back. "I..." she looked away, biting her lip. "I can't seem to help myself. I do care for him."

"And that's a problem?"

"He..."

How to say it? Dare she say it? William and Bennett were friends. No doubt William would take exception to her suspicion. Even if he'd seen the signs of what Bennett had become, his friendship could have blinded him to the truth. A rush of emotion closed over her throat and filled her eyes with tears. How cruel was fate to have brought home the only man she'd ever loved, and then hold him forever out of reach...unless she'd be willing to embrace the darkness with him and become one of the living dead.

"Em?" He covered her hand with his warm palm. Warm, not cold like Bennett's.

In a strangled whisper she said, "He's changed."

"He's the same in all the ways that matter."

"More than that. Much more than that."

"Tell me."

Very well. She'd tell him and come what may. She stood and drew a steadying breath. "Walk with me?"

William stood and offered his arm. As they slowly walked the perimeter of the room, William matching his pace to match Emma's, she tried to organize her thoughts but failed miserably.

"You're limping," William said. "Are you hurt?"

"Just my ankle."

"Here then." He guided her to a settee underneath a large window overlooking the garden.

The other callers' voices rose and fell, underscored by laughter and the rustling of clothing and feet. Mama's trilling laughter wove in through it all. In a low voice no one else would overhear, she spilled out the whole story in broken fragments and out of order. William listened without comment until she'd finished.

She took his offered handkerchief and wiped an errant tear. "But now I'm so confused because he really hasn't changed that much but yet he's changed in the most awful way, but I still love him and it hurts me deeply." She ended on a sob that she muffled with the handkerchief.

His voice was incredulous. "You honestly believe this, don't you?"

The roughness in his voice might have been his attempt to quell his laughter, or anger, or disbelief. She couldn't be certain. If she'd been able to see through her tears, she would have known by his expression. "After everything I've told you, how can you not?"

"Because he's a friend and I won't believe the worst of him because of a few strange events."

As tears streamed down her cheeks, she turned toward a window and pretended to admire the view of the gardens so others in the room wouldn't see. "I don't want to believe it, either. Truly I don't."

"Look, as much as it pains me to see how much you still love him, I won't encourage this mad fantasy you've created about him."

"Pains you? Why would it pain you?"

He let out a humorless laugh. "Because, my dear, you appear to be completely blind to that fact that I've loved you even longer than you've loved him."

Speechless, she could only stare.

William's mouth twisted into a humorless smile.

She shook her head slowly. "I...I had no idea. Why didn't you tell me?"

"I vowed I'd wait until Ashton came home from the war to give him a chance. It seemed only fair, considering the sacrifices he made to serve king and country."

"Oh, William..."

# *Emma's Dilemma*

"So as much as I'd love to prey on your lovably over-active imagination and beg you to marry me rather than the dreadful vampire, I refuse to win you in that manner. The question is; what are you going to do?"

She wrapped her arms around herself. "I don't know. I can't bear to see him harmed. But I also cannot stand by and allow him to hurt others, even if he needs it to survive."

William waited.

Emma bit her lip, trying to think. "Perhaps he could go away, somewhere safe?"

But where would he go? People whose blood he needed would never be safe, and he'd always risk detection, a mob, a stake through the heart.

Shuddering, Emma pressed her hands over her face. "This is all so complicated. And what if he wants to feed on me? Or transform me?"

"What if he does?"

Tears began anew. "I don't know. I can't be one of *them*."

"Do you love him?"

"Yes," she moaned. "Heaven help me, I do."

He stared out the window. "Then the choice should be easy. Place your heart in his hands and trust him."

She sniffed. "I had no idea you were such a romantic."

"For all the good it's doing me," he grumbled.

"I'm sorry, William. Truly." She placed a hand on his arm.

He remained rigid, staring out. "I know." Finally, he turned to her. "Be happy, Emma. And consider carefully. He's suffered much. He deserves happiness, and he believes only you can help him find it." He kissed the back of her hand over her glove and strode away with his head high.

Her thoughts trailed after him a few moments, turning over what might have been. Immediately they returned to Bennett. If he truly wanted her, he might do one of three things: marry her and protect her from himself; lose control some night and feed off her; or worse, transform her into a vampire. A myth she'd read in the lending library on folklore suggested some vampires could feed off of humans without killing them, but other myths said vampires always drained their victims, resulting in death.

Had Bennett changed so much that he'd do that to her?

She replayed their time together in the garden, and then today when he called. Nothing about him suggested any evil intentions. He seemed a more sober version of the Bennett she'd always known and loved, still as thoughtful and gentle as ever.

William was right. If she loved Bennett, she must also trust him. Love was meaningless without trust.

# Chapter 5

Emma spent the following morning agonizing over Bennett to Millie. At first, Millie opened her mouth in shocked silence and just stared.

"You think me mad," Emma said between her tears.

"How can you even consider spending time with a vampire?"

"I know," Emma wailed. "But I love him. Everything I loved about him is still there. His subtle wit, his gentleness, his goodness. Being a vampire hasn't taken away any of that."

"Emma, he kills people!"

"I don't know that. Maybe he's one of those vampires who only takes what he must have to survive and leaves his victims alive."

"No, you can't think of this. I can't stand the thought of you getting hurt."

"He won't hurt me."

"How can you know that?"

"Well..." How to explain it? "He didn't last night

at the ball. He could have and no one would have been the wiser."

"There might have been witnesses."

"No, we were alone."

Millie let out a long-suffering sigh. "I'm coming back tonight with cloves of garlic and I'm going to sleep in your room with you so he doesn't come and spirit you away or drink your blood."

Emma burst into tears. "Oh, Millie. I wish it weren't true. I don't know what to do."

Millie wrapped her arms around her and held her while she wept. "There, there. We'll think of something."

Emma rested against her friend's shoulder, letting her warmth and friendship soothe her. "I agreed to go driving with him today. Nothing can happen while we're in an open curricle. In fact, I need to get ready. I must look a fright." She pulled out of Millie's arms and straightened.

Millie rose and headed for the door. "Be careful, Emma. I hope you know what you're doing."

She hoped she knew was she was doing, too.

Bennett arrived at exactly the most fashionable hour to go driving at Hyde Park where one could see and be seen by the *beau monde*. Impeccably dressed in a royal blue frockcoat, a pair of cream knit pantaloons that hugged his well-formed body, and gleaming riding boots, he waited for her in the foyer. Emma nervously fingered the top button of her plum pelisse she'd put on over her afternoon gown as she limped to him from the front parlor.

He smiled brilliantly. Emma's heart flipped over. Would she ever get used to that smile? And more importantly, did she dare risk all to see it every day of her life?

"Emma, you look positively radiant." He stripped off his right glove, took her gloved hand, and pressed a kiss to it.

Heartily wishing she hadn't yet donned her kidskin gloves so she could feel his touch on her skin, she quashed the voice of reason that suggested it was best she not feel his cold lips. She returned his smile. "You look dashing, too."

In fact, he looked quite well. He appeared to have more color in his face. Was that a result of a recent feeding? She shook off the thought. They were going driving together and she refused to think about his dark secret. Today, she would enjoy herself.

"How is your ankle?" he asked. "You're still limping."

"Better, thank you."

As they stepped out into the sunshine, he donned his unusual darkened sunglasses.

She paused at the top of the front steps. "Oh, dear. More stairs. Those are the worst. It took me half the morning to get downstairs from my room."

He halted at the top, eyeing the steps. "Lean on me, and while you hold onto the railing, step down with your injured foot."

She did as he direct. The pain wasn't as bad as she'd feared.

"Now, bring the other one to that same step and shift your weight onto the good leg."

"It worked." She beamed up at him. "That didn't hurt much at all."

She repeated the process until they were down the stairs to the street. He led her to a gleaming new curricle drawn by a pair of beautiful, matched bays.

"Oh, my how lovely. Just look at those legs. And their eyes! I can always spot an intelligent horse by the placement of his eyes. They're beautiful, Bennett!"

Grinning, he affected a brief bow. "I'm so glad to have won the approval of the most horse-mad girl in London."

She giggled. Grinning, he lifted her carefully into the carriage, holding her steady until she was situated comfortably in the open carriage. He was steady, sure, strong. He held her gaze for a long moment, his open affection so pure and sincere that her throat tightened. She felt completely safe with him. She *was* safe with him, she no longer doubted that. There was nothing evil about this man, no matter what had happened to him.

After a quick snap of the reins, they were off, chatting about horses as he skillfully guided the carriage through the busy streets of London. She admired his profile and watched the sunlight gleam on his raven hair. How wonderful it was to have him back in her life! How much she'd missed him!

Wait. Sunlight? She looked up and squinted. The sun shone. Although Bennett wore his strange darkened glasses and his hat pulled down low, he was still out in direct sunlight. How could that be possible?

Their pace slowed once they reached the park and all her thoughts of his being a vampire momentarily fled. They enjoyed greeting friends, renewing acquaintances. More than once, she caught looks of envy tossed her way by young misses who'd hoped to capture the interest of the handsome Bennett Ashton, and she couldn't help but sit up a little straighter and smile smugly.

They greeted an old acquaintance who proudly showed off her new collie sitting regally next to her on the seat. Emma smiled, remembering a childhood prank gone wrong that involved a collie.

As they ended their conversation and Bennett moved the carriage forward, he smiled sideways at Emma. "Remember when we snuck in through the window at the spinster's house to see if she really did have a wooden leg?"

Emma laughed. "I was just thinking the same thing—her collie chased us off!"

Nodding, he chuckled. "That nasty dog tore a hole in my breeches."

Emma giggled and put a hand over her face at the memory of Bennett's smallclothes peeking out from the hole. He'd been two parts sheepish and one part indignant.

"My father took exception to my coming home in such a fashion." Bennett winced as if remembering his father's punishment. "But I suppose I deserved it."

"It was a naughty thing for us to do," Emma agreed.

"We never found out about her leg," he mused.

"I did. She does have a wooden leg. Apparently, she had a terrible sickness in it when she was but a child and the surgeon had to remove her whole leg or she would have died. Poor thing. I almost burst into tears when I found out about it."

As usual, Bennett listened intently as if she were the only person in the world. His expression grew very soft. "I love how deeply you feel everything."

"You don't find me silly and dramatic?"

"I find you passionate and vivacious."

Her heart swelled and she wanted to throw her arms around him.

All too soon, the afternoon ended and he turned his carriage around to take her home. In front of her family's London house, she leaned on his arm as she took the stairs up, repeating the process in reverse. Inside the doorway, he gave her arm a tug and pulled her into a recess where they wouldn't be seen. He swept her into his arms. She let out a little gasp at his bold move.

"Blast these things." He tore off his darkened glasses, and tossed them aside. "Now I can see you better."

She looked up at him while her heart throbbed. The excitement of being in his arms far surpassed her imagination. A moment later, his gloves came off and he dropped them on the floor behind her as he pulled her into him. His nearness shot little quivers down to her toes.

"Emma, I promised myself I'd take this slowly. I know we've been apart a long time, and I know we've changed over the time we were apart, so I didn't want to rush you. But you are the reason I'm alive. Thoughts of you kept me warm during those dark times, those cold nights, those hours when I thought I'd die. I got hurt and sick more than once while I was away, and each time I fought my way back because I had to come home to you."

She forgot how to breathe. Her gaze remained fixed on him, heart pounding in her ears and the earlier tingles turning into rapids.

"I can't bear to wait another moment. I want you in my life and in my arms every moment of every day. Marry me, Emma. I'm not perfect, and I'm not sure I'll ever fully recover from what I suffered in the war, but I vow to do everything I can to make you happy. I love you. Please, will you have me?"

Tears welled up in her eyes until his face faded into swirls of light and dark. As tears trickled down her face, she nodded. "I love you, too. Yes, I'll marry you. Of course I will. I've been waiting for you for years to ask me that question."

He laughed and pulled her in tighter. Slowly, he leaned his head down, closer, closer, until she thought she'd faint from anticipation. He kissed her gently, softly, and oh, so tenderly. Every nerve in her body sprang to life. She kissed him with an eagerness that surprised her. He responded, his tenderness evaporating into hunger and he devoured her lips as if he were starving. Her knees wobbled, and he tightened his grip until she could hardly breathe.

She soared into a realm of joy. She buried her roots deeper into a sense of permanency.

She was safe. She was home. Bennett was here with her, and nothing else mattered.

When he finally released her, he pressed her against his chest and kissed the top of her head. He let out a pained groan, his breathing ragged. "I'd best find your father fast and ask his permission lest I give into temptation to ravish you right here."

She laughed weakly.

He cupped her cheek and kissed her again, carefully guiding his passion back to his previous tenderness. After ending the kiss, he buried his face in her neck. "Oh, how I love you."

As he pulled back to look at her, she smiled up at him and traced his cheek with her fingers. Her other hand rested on his broad chest right over his heart which beat as rapidly as hers.

Then, it dawned on her.

His heart beat under her hand, hard and steady. Heat seeped into her skin from his face.

He was warm.

Warm!

He couldn't be a vampire if he had a heartbeat and was warm. Then, that meant...she'd been wrong about him.

He wasn't a vampire.

Oh happy day! Relief flooded her with such force that her knees wobbled. Her heart nearly leaped out of her chest and she wanted to sing and dance in pure joy.

But what about all those things that had led her to believe he was a vampire?

He chuckled softly. "What is it? You have the most adorable little frown on your face." He kissed the tip of her nose with his warm, soft lips.

Her face hot with embarrassment, she laughed softly and bit her lip. "Ahhhh, you're not going to like this, but er...well, for a while, I actually thought..." she cleared her throat feeling supremely childish. "I though you might have been...well...a vampire."

He blinked. "A what?"

"You know, a vampire, like in the legends."

He pulled away a little, looking at her as if she'd grown a second nose. "You jest."

"No, I'm in earnest."

He shook his head, his brow forming a crease, and let out a half laugh. "Wha...?"

"Oh, dear, it all sounds so ridiculous now. But whole time I was absolutely miserable because I thought I'd truly lost you."

A slow smile curved his lips. "You read that

vampire book all the young ladies are talking about, didn't you?"

She ducked her head. "*Miss Vernon and the Vampire*. Yes. And I admit, that may have been what planted the seed of the idea in my head. But I thought I'd found so much evidence that I couldn't doubt."

He led her to a divan in the front parlor, keeping the door properly open, and sat her down. He sank next to her. "What evidence?"

"Well..." she moistened her lips. "When you kissed my hand at the Smythe-Buchanan's party, you were cold. Ice cold."

His eyes took on a faraway look as if remembering the details of that day. "At the garden party? I'd just eaten an ice, which was silly because it was such a chilly day. It made me cold through and through."

"So, your hands and your mouth were cold from the ice."

"Numb, in fact, and I realized I was speaking strangely because my mouth was a little numb, too. When you looked at me so oddly, I wondered if I sounded worse than I thought."

"And you were so pale. *Are* so pale"

He nodded. "I've been ill. Did I mention that?"

"Yes, but I thought you were referring to your transformation as an illness."

He smiled and kissed first her brow, then her temple with his warm, warm mouth. "You really do have a vivid imagination. No, I had scarlet fever. I was ill for a long time. I nearly died, I'm told."

She drew in a breath at the thought of him dying and touched his face. "I wish you'd sent me word."

"There was nothing you could have done. And I would never risk exposing you to such a serious illness."

"Still, to have been kept in the dark about how bad off you were..." She gripped his hands. "Bennett, you mustn't keep shutting me out like that. I need to be a part of your life, the good as well as the bad."

"I know that now. It does make the burden lighter." He pulled her in close to him.

She rested her head on his shoulder. "Why do you wear darkened glasses?"

"The fever settled into my eyes. I fear I don't see as well as I once did, and my eyes are very sensitive to bright light." He cupped her cheek with his hand and smiled down at her tenderly. "What else made you believe I was a vampire? Surely, those weren't the only things."

"No, I also noticed there were no mirrors at your house."

"There are mirrors." He narrowed his eyes in thought. "The large mirror in the foyer got broken recently. I believe it was just before you and your mother came calling. My mother has since replaced it."

"And I saw you in the graveyard in the middle of the night."

"Graveyard?" His eyes moved as if viewing a scene from the past. "Oh, yes, I've been taking a flower to the grave of a friend every Monday. He saved my life on the battlefield. I'd remembered after dinner that I'd neglected to do that, so I went rather later than usual. It's actually quite peaceful at night."

"And I suppose that night you and I were in the garden at the ball—the night I twisted my ankle—it was a mere coincidence that a bat flew behind the bushes and you walked out the other way."

He chuckled. "I was sitting there, enjoying a moment of quiet, when the bat nearly bumped into me. I jerked out of the way and decided I'd had enough of the cold night air. I was returning to the party when I came upon you."

She nodded silently. How could she have let her imagination rule her head and her heart like that?

He smiled and traced her cheek. "Besides, so many couples had walked past and found a quiet spot to be together, that I'd begun to feel rather lonely. I went to seek you out. Then, there you were."

She let out her breath in self-deprecating amusement. "I was terrified. I thought the bat was you."

"So you ran and fell and twisted your ankle, all because you thought I was going to pounce on you and drink your blood." He grinned wickedly. "I admit, I'm a little glad. I got to pick you up and hold you in my arms."

"You touched me so gently I'd almost decided right then and there I didn't care if you were a vampire. I loved you even more than I did before you left."

His smile faded and he blinked slowly at her. "So you accepted my proposal, all the time believing this of me?"

Silently, she nodded.

"Oh, Em. You were really willing to take that chance?"

"I trust you. I know you'd never hurt me. And if you decided to change me into a vampire, then we'd be together for all eternity."

"We will. But we'll start as mortals, and finish it in Heaven."

"That sounds perfect."

"Are you disappointed I'm just an ordinary man?"

She put and hand on either side of his face and gaze up at him with all the love in her heart. "Nothing about you is ordinary. You've always been remarkable."

A devilish light danced in his dark eyes. "Very well, I confess; I really am a vampire. Prepare to become my victim." He pounced on her, knocking her over onto the soft cushions on the divan, and proceeded to kiss and nibble her neck.

Giggling, she shivered as pleasure rippled over her skin everywhere his mouth touched her. As he kissed her lips again, possessively, tenderly, she knew their love would transcend all time. And they would fill the darkness with warmth and love.

The End

# CONSTANT HEARTS

*Inspired by Jane Austen's Persuasion*

# Chapter 1

London, 1815

The last person Amelia planned to see at the soiree was Reed St. Ives, and she certainly didn't expect to see him leaning over the hostess's unconscious body. Her heart stalled, then beat an unsteady rhythm. Reed drew every light in the drawing room as if the sun's rays shone on him. Broader now, even more handsome than before, and with a more confident air, Reed's power over her had not faded with the passing years.

"Stand back," Reed said. "Someone open a window."

Obedient to Reed's command, the crowd stepped back and threw open windows. With a guilty start, Amelia remembered her friend Lady Evensley lying in a swoon and tried to turn her attention to its proper focus. Reed checked Lady Evensley's pulse with his long, slender fingers. He'd always had such lovely hands—masculine, yet graceful—the hands of the

101

gifted pianist. Years ago, those fingers had traced Amelia's cheek with utmost gentleness. She shivered. Best not to dwell on that, or on what might have been.

In spite of Reed's directive, Amelia stepped closer, eyeing Lady Evensley's pallid face, and began fanning her. Lord Evensley knelt next to his wife, his gaze flitting frantically between her face and Reed's. "I've never seen her faint."

"It's probably just the heat," came Reed's assuring voice as his dark head bent over the lady. "Her pulse is strong and she's breathing freely. Bring me a damp cloth." He began chaffing her wrists as a footman dashed out of the room.

Amelia turned to her aunt. "Your vinaigrette, Aunt."

"Oh, yes, of course." Aunt Millie handed over her small silver box containing a vinegar-soaked sponge.

Amelia stepped forward and leaned down, accidentally brushing against Reed's arm. Heat flared across her skin and her senses filled with his scent. His very presence sent a wave of longing over her. As she held out the vinaigrette, she swallowed and forced her words through a dry throat. "Perhaps this will help revive her?"

"Thank you." Without glancing at Amelia, Reed took the delicately carved box out of her hand and flicked open the hinged lid, releasing the pungent smell of vinegar. He waved it under the nostrils of Lady Evensley.

Amelia swallowed her stung pride that he hadn't noticed her—just as well since they were entirely unsuitable for a number of reasons. Or so she'd told herself all those years ago. And every day since.

Lady Evensley's eyes fluttered. "Oh, my. I hope I haven't ruined the party."

"Not at all, my dear." Lord Evensley helped her sit up.

Amelia added wickedly, "Merely added a bit of spice to the evening. Although, next time you'll have to outdo this one. Perhaps invite a few pirates?"

Lady Evensley laughed softly. "I just might at that. Know any?"

"I'll be sure to make introductions if I cross paths with one." They shared a smile.

Reed returned the vinaigrette to Amelia. "Thank you..." He broke off as his gaze found hers, and the color faded from his face. His voice sounded hoarse when he spoke. "Amy."

Bathed in the warmth of his golden-green gaze, Amelia found it difficult to breathe. His face had matured. Its chiseled lines were more rugged, his jaw more square. His hair was the same rich mahogany, shorter than he used to wear it, but just as thick. A white scar bisected his chin, a new flaw that somehow enhanced his masculinity. His hazel eyes, both green and golden brown, searched hers with the desperation of a drowning man reaching for a lifeline. Those eyes had once been filled with wide-eyed dreaminess, but now held something almost...haunted.

She stretched a hand toward him and her voice fled, leaving only a whisper, "Reed."

Visibly remembering himself, he cleared his throat and inclined his head. "Madam."

His formality came as a sharp reminder of what had passed between them, and what they had lost. Or rather, what she had thrown away.

She folded her hands together. "Good evening."

A shadow passed over his face, and he recoiled as if her presence repelled him. His gaze took in her silk evening gown and rubies in her hair. "You're looking...well." His tone made it sound like an insult. In a clear cut, he turned back to his patient and helped her to stand.

Stunned, Amelia arose. She should step back but found herself unable to move. Whatever familiar affection she'd expected to find in his gaze was decidedly absent. She'd feared to discover traces of lingering hurt—after all, she'd broken his heart—but

104

she'd never dreamed she'd find such coldness. A low murmur began as the crowd lost interest now that their hostess had revived. With any luck, few of them knew of Amelia's prior relationship to Reed, thus sparing her of further gossip.

Reed focused on the hostess. "How do you feel, my lady?"

"Ridiculous. I never swoon." Lady Evensley stood, swayed momentarily and then straightened. She lifted her gaze to her guests. "I believe dinner is served."

"Quite right." Amelia made a grand gesture to the dining room to get the guests moving and spare Lady Evensley further embarrassment. No one questioned her authority to direct the crowd and the soft murmur of voices rose in crescendo as the guests filed into the dining room.

A gentleman appeared at Amelia's side. "Shall we?" Amelia blinked at him, belatedly remembering he'd been introduced as her dinner escort. "Of course." She gathered her poise, offered him her brightest smile, and took his offered arm. "The pleasure would be mine." Against her will, her gaze returned to Reed.

He stood speaking softly to the host and hostess and flashed that self-deprecating grin she'd always found so charming.

She walked away from him, her heart tearing as deeply as it had when she'd walked away from him— had it been six years go? It seemed a lifetime ago, and yet, as painful as if it had only been days. Clenching the arm of her escort lest she crumple, Amelia moved with the other guests into the dining room. All feeling left her body except for the tearing of her heart.

She'd been a fool to think herself over him. She'd been a fool to imagine he'd still care for her after all these years. But most of all, she'd been a fool to reject him when he'd wanted her.

Amelia bit her lip. It was just as well. Nothing had changed; they were no better suited now than they were when she'd rejected him to honor her uncle's wishes. She shuddered in a breath, but couldn't make her lungs fill. After finding her place, she sank into a seat between two distinguished gentlemen who were both attentive and courteous—a miracle really, considering the scandal surrounding her. No doubt Lady Evensley had made that considerate arrangement.

"Are you enjoying the season?" Amelia asked her dinner companion.

"I certainly am. Although I admit, the house party I attended last week was far more diverting than most of these dinner parties and balls in London."

"The Duke of Suttenberg's house party?"

"The same."

"Ah. Do you ride to hounds, then?" Amelia fixed her gaze upon his face lest she be tempted to look for Reed like some lovesick puppy.

"Jolly good time. The hounds chased the fox up a tree."

Amelia raised a brow. "Indeed? The duke's hounds climb trees? How very clever of them."

He chuckled. "The tree had fallen, and lay against other trees in the woods at a fair angle, but that makes for a good story, does it not?"

She laughed. "It certainly does."

"And you? Are you enjoying London?"

Ah. The question she'd hoped he'd ask. "Very much, although I admit I have a bit of an ulterior motive for coming this season."

"Oh? Husband hunting, are you?"

She sniffed. "Certainly not. I'm here seeking funding for improvements I wish to make at an orphanage."

"Orphanage?"

"The conditions last winter were so bad that more than three fourths of the children died of typhus. That's a higher rate than those who die of gaol fever in Newgate."

"'Pon my word."

"It's simply intolerable. So I demanded that those in authority be replaced and I'm personally supervising—and funding—necessary changes. Unfortunately, purchasing enough decent food for a whole houseful of orphans, not to mention improving their conditions, is very expensive, so I'm looking for new ways to locate sources of financial means. And the board of directors is being extremely cautious." She sighed helplessly, secretly waiting to see if he'd taken the bait.

His eyes took on a faraway look. "I'm an orphan. Fortunately for me, my grandparents took me in. I could have been one of those with no family."

She nodded. Lady Evensley had apparently taken great pains with her seating arrangements. "You are, indeed, fortunate you had family to care for you. Think of all those poor little ones with nowhere to go."

"Perhaps I could help." She fixed a gaze of adoration upon him and let out a happy sigh.

"Oh, that would be wonderful!" She reached into her reticule. "Here's my card. Do call upon me and let's discuss the particulars. I would be most grateful for your assistance."

"Of course."

Amelia tried not to gloat. Perhaps this plan

would be easier than she thought. Thanks to Aunt Millie, and Lord and Lady Evensley, her re-entrée to society might work after all for the benefit of the children.

During the lull in conversation, Reed's rich laugh rang out, drawing her gaze. He smiled at his dinner companion as if he hadn't a care. Appalling, really, how all those old feelings resurfaced, feelings better left buried. Yet with vicious intensity, memories played out in her mind; Reed laughing with the sun shining in his hair, the long, loving glances he used to cast her way from across the room, his fingers dancing on the pianoforte while his lovely baritone rang out, his compassion for all God's creatures, his reckless streak whenever he rode a horse. If only he'd come from a family of which Aunt and Uncle approved!

Amelia cast a guilty glance at Aunt Millie across the table. Yet, at the moment, Amelia had trouble remembering why it would have been so bad to be the wife of a gentle surgeon whose grandfather owned a factory. There were worse things. Her gaze shifted to him again and Reed caught her stare. His expression hard, he silently raised a glass to her in mocking homage.

Amelia focused on eating, though she barely tasted the food. He despised her; that much was clear.

And she couldn't blame him. If he'd rejected her for such shallow reasons as dowry or family status, she would have hated him, too. Besides, she was used to scorn; many of her old friends, except the Evensleys, rejected her due to her public and scandalous divorce. Most days she despised herself, but not for the reason people would suppose. She continued speaking with the men next to her, charming them with all her skill in the hopes they'd be generous in their sponsorship of the orphanage. At the conclusion of the meal, she filed out with the ladies to leave the men to their conversation.

In the drawing room, one of the guests sat down at the harp. The sweet melody filled Amelia with a welcome calm. As a child Amelia had lain in her bedroom listening to her mother play the harp. The notes had sung to her in a tender lullaby. Amelia smiled at the memory.

Aunt Millie joined her on the settee. "Dr. St. Ives seems to have weathered the war well enough."

"Indeed." Amelia bit her lip.

Aunt Millie patted her hand and lowered her voice. "Don't worry, my dear. It's only natural for some of your old feelings to return at the first sight of a former love. It does get better."

If only it were that simple! Amelia looked up into the dear face of her namesake. "Did it happen to you?"

"Oh, yes. Each time I saw an old suitor for the first time, I had a bit of a shock. I always remembered what I adored about that particular young man. But it fades in time."

"It's been six years. It doesn't appear to have faded." Aunt Millie squeezed her hand, her eyes filled with empathy. "Perhaps mine faded because I was so happy with your uncle, God rest his soul."

Amelia wished she'd had the spine to follow her heart. But she hadn't dared. Besides, it was too late now. And really, there was no way of knowing truly what might have been. She doubted she would have been content to remain in England while Reed went off to war. Nor could she imagine going with him to live the life of a soldier's wife, witnessing the horrors of battle.

Instead she had trusted Aunt and Uncle's judgment, and found ridicule, scandal, rejection, heartache in marriage to a different man. She'd faced her own private battle, her own private horrors. She'd faced them alone, without Reed's strong, comforting presence. Following the drum at his side may not have been as bad. At least they would have had each other. Shaking off her dark memories, Amelia glanced at the Lady Evensley who looked fully recovered. Still, it would be polite to inquire as to her health.

"Excuse me, Aunt." She arose and crossed the room to her friend. "Are you feeling better?"

"Oh, my goodness, yes. I can't imagine what came over me." Saucily, Amelia said, "One sherry too many, perhaps?"

"Perhaps." Lady Evensley lowered her gaze, blushing deeply.

Amelia suspected the lady was in a family way, yet she knew better than to ask such a personal question, even of a friend. After all, they'd only known each other a couple of years. "It was fortunate Dr. St. Ives was nearby to aid you."

Lady Evensley smiled. "Such a kind man. Are you acquainted with him?"

"Yes, I met him before he went away to the war."

"I understand he was the private surgeon for a general. Quite well respected—for a surgeon, that is."

Amelia winced at yet another reminder about the unsuitability of a low-born surgeon marrying the daughter of a lord. Her voice came out a bit strangled. "I believe you are correct. It's difficult not to respect him once one gets to know him. How do you know Dr. St Ives?"

"He and my husband became friends during the war—an unlikely friendship, to be sure, which only speaks volumes about the character of Dr. St. Ives."

Lady Evensley let out a sigh. "I'm so glad my dear one is home well and whole."

Amelia's heart swelled with sympathy. "I know you are. I cannot believe how well you managed without him."

"It wasn't easy, I assure you. I'd like to give that horrible Napoleon a piece of my mind for all the mischief he caused."

Amelia hid a smile, unsure if 'mischief' was quite the right word for years of war and bloodshed the Corsican Monster caused.

Lady Evensley glanced sideways at Amelia, her eyes twinkling. "The good doctor is uncommonly handsome, and my husband couldn't say enough about him. I am persuaded that plenty of young ladies might be willing to overlook his low family connections to make such a match."

"Perhaps." Amelia hoped her voice did not betray her, but feared her expression already had. She'd never been good at disguising her thoughts. The gentlemen eventually joined them, and they all began a game of charades. Despite her earlier vow to avoid watching Reed, he drew her gaze as he laughed and interacted with the other guests who'd unquestioningly accepted him into their elite circle. They might have done it for the host's sake, but more likely because of Reed's infectious charm. Reed never glanced her way. Either he was ignoring her deliberately, or had absolutely no feelings for her whatsoever. She shifted her position so that another guest blocked her view of him. Best not to look at temptation.

Lady Evensley stood. "I know this may sound juvenile, but let's play a game of hide and seek. We played it at the duchess's party Tuesday past, and it was ever so much fun."

Exclamations of delight followed this announcement and there was a flurry of activity as people fled the room in search of hiding places. Amelia was tempted to plead fatigue and return home, thus sparing herself further anguish of Reed's presence. Yet she found herself reluctant to leave, probably out of some bizarre desire to further inflict pain upon herself by vainly watching for Reed while he continued to ignore her. The unconcealed pain in his eyes as she'd declared them unsuitable years ago haunted her even now. No doubt that pain turned into resentment and eventually hatred. Perhaps he'd moved on, loved another woman, and forgotten all they once had. The thought pierced her heart like an arrow.

She should leave. Remaining here only reopened old wounds. Besides, her work here was done. She'd gotten both of her dinner companions to agree to meet with her to discuss helping fund the orphanage. After scanning the emptying room, she found Aunt Millie, virtually sparkling, something she rarely did since Uncle had died. Amelia curled her hands into fists. It would be selfish to ask

Aunt Millie to leave. Amelia could hire a hack and return home alone of course, but shivered at the thought of doing so this late at night. Very well, a game of hide and seek. She could find a hiding place that would ensure she wouldn't be found, and enjoy some solitude.

Amelia went to the library. Inside, she waited to let her vision adjust to the dim lighting coming from only a few candles, then curled up between a sideboard table and a display case behind a divan, looking forward to time away from all pretenses.

"Well." Something warm touched her back. Stifling a cry, Amelia turned her head. Her breath left in a whoosh. "Reed."

# Chapter 2

Reed stared at Amy kneeling within reach, his heart hammering against his ribs. She was even lovelier than before, with a fuller, riper figure, and skin still as smooth as a child's. She sat as if rooted to the floor, her eyes darting between his like they once did when trying to divine his thoughts. Wariness had replaced their trusting innocence of bygone years. He fisted his hands lest he do something stupid, like shake her shoulders and shout. Or haul her against him and kiss her until the years melted away.

"Forgive me," she said breathlessly. "I didn't realize anyone else was here."

"Sorry to disappoint." He didn't bother to keep the sarcasm out of his voice.

She stilled. "I'll leave."

"Perhaps that would be best."

She didn't move.

Neither did he.

Bound in a spell woven around them, they sat on the floor of the library locked in each other's gaze. The

116

air crackled with the kind of electricity that comes with a thunderstorm. His focus fell to that luscious mouth that had tempted him years ago, lips she'd said were too full but which he'd always found utterly delicious. Her perfume curled around him, a heady blend of innocent rose and seductive jasmine.

"Amy," he whispered. Caught by an irresistible force, Reed touched her smooth cheek, caressing back and forth, then he cradled her face in his hands. She closed her eyes and tilted her face up toward his. So tempting, so lovely. He leaned in and brushed his mouth over hers. Tingles spread outward, immersing him in a long-absent warmth. She let out a tiny sigh. He lowered his head and kissed her again, tugging gently. Her lips, unbearably soft and welcoming, filled him with intoxicating desire. As warmth turned to aching heat, he devoured her mouth, pouring out long-suppressed passion.

She slid her arms around him, one hand touching that sensitive place at the back of his neck. He crushed her to him as their mouths sought to regain the lost years, to repair broken hearts and shattered dreams. Laughter and voices outside the door brought Reed back to consciousness. He ended the kiss and pulled away.

Without her in his arms, cold seeped into his soul.

117

Her moist and swollen lips parted, and she let out a sob. A tear fell from each eye. Reed watched, mesmerized, as they trickled down her cheeks. How had he hurt her?

"Oh, how I've missed you," she whispered.

Reed almost cursed out loud. He'd just opened himself up to further pain and rejection by the very women who'd nearly destroyed him years ago, a mistake he would not make a second time. Reed snapped his head back and looked down at her with contempt. "Really? Was that before or after you raced to the altar with another man?"

She flinched at his venomous tone. Another tear fell. "Since I bade you farewell."

He summoned every drop of scorn in his voice that he could muster. All those long, lonely nights, those days without hope, the utter emptiness, surged through him in hot bitterness. "That was your choice, madam, not mine."

"I was trying to do the right thing. What could I do? I wasn't old enough to marry without Uncle's permission, and I couldn't bear the scandal of an elopement. I just...couldn't go against my family's wishes."

*I would have waited for you,* he wanted to shout, but he held his tongue. Betraying how badly his heart ached for her even now would not serve. It was ironic, really, that she'd wished to avoid scandal by marrying him, only to find it with the man she'd married.

"So you wed someone of whom your uncle approved. Have you ever regretted that?"

The bloom faded from her cheeks. "Daily. From the beginning." She lifted her chin and a hard glint came into her eyes. "No doubt you heard about my divorce."

"I did." The papers had spared no detail of the whole ugly affair.

"I suppose you think I received what I deserved."

No one deserved what she'd received, but Reed fortified the barrier around his heart. "You might have regretted marrying me as well. Following the drum is a hard life. At least with him, you had everything money could buy. And you had your precious social approval." He stood. "I'll find another hiding place and leave you this one."

He left the library and closed the door behind him. In the next room, he leaned against the door, trying to remember to breathe, and pressed the heels of his shaking hands into his eyes. The shock of seeing Amy again left his insides swirling in a chaotic maelstrom. She was just as beautiful, but heartache had left its mark upon her. The shadow in her eyes reflected the same look he'd seen on countless wounded men brought in from the battlefield. Though he'd been the personal surgeon of a general on the peninsula, he'd lent a hand after each battle rather than sitting idly by and watching men suffer as they waited to receive medical aid. He'd seen more human misery than he'd ever thought possible. To find that same misery in Amy's eyes smote him to the heart.

Reed pushed off from the door and made himself walk across the room. He'd left another piece of his heart in the library, but refused to go back in there. She'd rejected him years ago. He wouldn't give her the pleasure of doing it again. But, as he already knew too well, resentment was a cold bedfellow, and he feared he'd never be warm again.

# Chapter 3

Amelia paused, her fork suspended halfway to her mouth, and blinked across the breakfast table at her aunt. "You want me to what?"

"Ask Dr. St. Ives for a sleep remedy for me." Amelia let out an un-lady-like snort. Likely, the only cure Aunt Millie sought was one for Amelia's wounded heart. "I'd hoped I'd heard you wrong. He's a surgeon, not a physician. Besides, if you're not sleeping well, ask your own doctor."

Aunt Millie made a dismissive wave. "My physician will just prescribe laudanum. I'm losing confidence in him. I want a fresh new opinion."

"Then seek another doctor in London." Amelia rubbed the space between her eyes. She couldn't bear the thought of giving Reed a new opportunity to reject her. "I have located five new sponsors for the orphanage, and have much to do."

Aunt Millie pouted. "I don't want to see another doctor. I want to hear what Dr. St. Ives has to say. Lady Evensley said he gave her some tea that made her sleep like a child, and I want some."

"Then ask him for it."

"I can't. I promised to help a friend with her guest list this morning, and this afternoon I'm meeting someone else at the museum. Tonight is the musicale. I simply haven't the time, and if I don't start getting a decent night's sleep, I'll develop bags under my eyes."

Amelia regarded her suspiciously. "You don't look as if you've been suffering from lack of sleep."

"I feel positively dreadful." Her tone revealed exactly the opposite. "Amelia, please? Won't you do this one thing for me?"

Aunt Millie gave her such sad, pleading eyes that Amelia let out a long-suffering sigh. She pushed away her plate without finishing her breakfast. "Very well. You make me feel a beast for refusing you."

Aunt Millie laughed softly. "I knew I could count on you, dearest." She delicately decorated her bread with jam as if she were working on a painting. "I hear he's staying at his brother's house. Do you know the place?"

"Yes, Aunt. But I feel positively manipulated."

Aunt Millie smiled. "I love you, too, dear."

"I'm to present the new plan to the board of directors at the orphanage this morning, so I'll pay a call to your new favorite doctor this afternoon. And hope he doesn't throw me out."

"You're such a dear." Aunt Millie stood and strode out with all the vigor of a person who'd just received the best night's sleep of her life.

Amelia dressed with special care in a rich, rose-colored gown, the shade Reed had once said made her glow with the beauty of Aphrodite. Then glared at her reflection. "I'm dressing to impress the board of directors, not to impress Reed."

The mirror made no comment.

With a groan of disgust, she turned away. She probably wouldn't even be allowed in the house long enough for him to see her clothing. She was such an idiot!

As she met with the board of directors, Amy firmly pushed back thoughts of Reed and focused instead on the children and her plans for the orphanage. She spoke passionately, with her head high, and firmly deflected any questions regarding her character, focusing instead on the business at hand. Her voice rang out with confidence. "I have secured enough funding to pay for my proposed changes for the next year. As far as the increase in food rations, I'm confident that the others with whom I've spoken will step forward and offer their support as well, so we'll have more than enough money to cover our expenses."

One of the gentlemen looked down at her with clear disapproval. Whether he disapproved of a woman in business, or found fault with her status as a divorcee, she didn't know, but she made a point of frequently looking at him in the eye as she discussed the reports and proposals. Whether or not she won them over for the remodeling project, she would still continue to improve conditions for the children, beginning with more quality food and warm bedding. If nothing else, she'd speak to her solicitor about selling some more assets and fund it herself.

She cleared her throat and passed out the papers. "Here are the itemized reports with past and proposed budgetary changes, as well as pledges I've received. I think you'll agree they are realistic." After she finished speaking, she clasped her hands together and waited for their decision.

The board of directors conferred, their voices a low hum. Amelia stood motionless while her insides twisted into a nervous knot.

Finally, the chairman nodded to her. "Very well, the majority has voted to approve your plan."

She resisted the urge to let out a squeal and jump up and down. She merely smiled. "Excellent. Thank you, gentlemen." Amelia wanted to sing out loud. She never would have tried to re-establish herself in society if she hadn't needed the aid for the orphanage so badly. But now, at last, she could affect true change for these children. With a firm sense of purpose, Amelia set out to meet with the contractor to begin improvements. If only she didn't have this meeting with Reed to endure!

# Chapter 4

Seated in the main gathering room inside Brooks's Gentleman's Club, Reed toyed with his glass and only half-listened to Lord Evensley. He scanned the club, admiring the architecture of the old building. As a guest of a peer, he'd been allowed into the exclusive club, but he'd never get in on his own merit. No matter. He'd never belonged to the beau monde, despite his parents' attempts to climb the elite ladders of society, nor did he care. Still, the good food and excellent port made the trip worthwhile.

A gentleman walking by stopped to chat. Remembering the gentleman from the dinner party the other night, Reed nodded a greeting, then narrowed his gaze. That had been the gentleman sitting next to Amelia, engrossed in conversation with her. How he'd envied that man! Reed shook himself. He wanted nothing to do with that rich, spoiled lord's daughter who thought she was too good for the likes of him.

The other gentleman sat. "I say, where have you been hiding that charming Amelia Dasherwood?"

Reed gave a little start.

Lord Evensley grinned. "You liked her, eh?"

"Lovely," said the gentleman. "And intelligent, too. I didn't think I'd find that combination so appealing. Have you heard about that orphanage she's sponsoring?"

Lord Evensley nodded. "Of course. We've already pledged our help."

Reed's ears perked. "Orphanage?"

"One that had a huge death toll last winter," Lord Evensley explained. "Mrs. Dasherwood has turned the place upside down making it more healthful for children."

The other gentleman nodded. "I went on a tour with her yesterday, and I must admit it was impossible not to get caught up in all the excitement. I dug deep into my pockets. But seeing her eyes light up was worth every shilling."

How well Reed recalled Amy's eyes all aglow.

"Hmmm," continued the other man. "Perhaps she'll let me court her now that she sees me so generous."

Reed glared at the man as he rhapsodized about Amy. She'd been his Amy. Or so he'd thought. But if she were funding an orphanage, she'd obviously matured since he'd seen her. Maybe status was no longer so important. It had been odd, really, how she'd seemed so in love with him, and then the moment her uncle refused his proposal, Amy had turned so cold. He'd thought she'd had more substance than that. An orphanage. Now that was worthwhile. Perhaps he could help. He could offer his services as a doctor to the children. But no, putting himself in Amy's path would lead nowhere he wished to go. Besides, he was leaving town soon and had no plans ever to return.

The other gentleman finally stopped yammering on about beautiful women on missions, and left.

"What is it about him you don't like?" Lord Evensley's voice broke in. Reed jumped.

"Eh? Oh, nothing. He seems a decent chap."

"You were positively glowering." Humor glittered his eyes.

"I meant no offense to your friend."

"Methinks you have designs upon Mrs. Dasherwood?" Lord Evensley raised a brow.

"No, of course not. Far above my class. I want nothing to do with lords' daughters. Too much trouble."

"Ah. You've asked about her, then."

"No. I already knew...." Reed closed his mouth with a snap.

Lord Evensley cocked his head and examined him while a smile played with his mouth. "A lady from the past?" He drew in a breath and snapped his fingers. "Of course. She's the lady from the past."

Reed scowled. "I never said anything about a lady from the past."

"When I first met you on the peninsula, you had the clear look of a man nursing a broken heart. Only a woman can leave a man in that kind of wreckage."

"I don't want to talk about it." Reed rubbed his eyes.

"Do you remember the night we got so drunk we got lost on the way back from that little tavern?" Lord Evensley asked.

Reed grinned. "After the brawl?"

"The same. You told me you envied me that I'd fallen for a woman who returned my affection. You refused to say anything more on the matter, but weeks later mentioned something about reaching above your class and getting your hand cut off."

"So now you know," Reed growled.

Lord Evernsley's voice took on a musing tone and he rubbed his chin slowly. "Mrs. Dasherwood went on to marry a real lout."

"It was her choice."

"Are you sure?"

Reed folded his arms. "Her uncle refused my suit and she coldly told me that her uncle knew best and that she couldn't see me ever again."

"How old was she?"

"Seventeen."

"Young. Impressionable."

"Unwilling to risk living on my means and social status."

Lord Evensley sipped his drink thoughtfully. "Is that why she refused you?"

"Look who she married. An Earl."

"Someone of whom her uncle approved." Evensly nodded sagely.

Reed toyed with a napkin. "You see?"

"Perhaps it was his approval that mattered. Going against the wishes of a guardian to whom she felt she owed her gratitude and obedience would have been difficult for any young lady."

"I begged her to elope."

"And disappoint her uncle, to say nothing of the scandal?" Evensly made a tsking sound. "I had no idea you had such an impetuous romantic side."

"Not any more. I've learned my lesson." Reed took out his watch and manufactured an escape. "I have an appointment. Thank you for inviting me here."

"Good afternoon." A knowing gleam remained in Lord Evensley's eye.

Reed left, mulling over his friend's words. Perhaps he'd asked too much of Amy, after all. Still, she'd married that earl only a few months later. Obviously their relationship had meant more to Reed than it had to Amy. If only he could forget her.

# Chapter 5

As nervous as a schoolgirl in the throws of her first *tendre*, Amelia smoothed the skirts of her pelisse. With her trembling hand poised over the knocker of the front door, she froze.

What was she doing? Reed clearly didn't want her back, despite the kiss they shared in the library. And what had that been about? There had been such longing in that kiss, such tenderness, such passion. Could it be possible he was still in love with her, but unwilling to allow her to see it? And yet, when he pushed her away, he'd looked at her as if she'd just insulted his honor.

More likely the kiss was merely a product of their close quarters and their shared loneliness, an act he instantly regretted because he despised her. Maybe he thought her unfit for him because she was divorced. Perhaps he'd become a complete rake and kissed every woman within reach.

No, that didn't seem at all like the man she'd known. Yet time changed people—would he have changed that much? So here she stood on the doorstep, blithely prepared to throw herself under his feet to see if he would pick her up or trample her. There must be something wrong with her, truly, if she were willing to subject herself to further suffering, notwithstanding her aunt's manufactured errand.

Gathering her courage, she knocked. After being admitted, Amelia waited, twisting her hands, in the front parlor while the butler went to inquire whether Dr. St. Ives was receiving visitors.

She didn't have to wait long. Immaculate in expertly tailored attire, Reed appeared. She tried not to notice how beautifully his bottle-green frockcoat fit his shoulders and set off his eyes, or how his cravat managed to look both Corinthian and careless. Most of all, she tried not to admire his intensely handsome face. She swallowed against a suddenly very dry mouth, an effect he seemed to always have on her.

He raised his brows but his face remained completely expressionless. "Good morning, madam."

Eyeing him uncertainly, she managed, "Why such formality, Reed?"

"I thought it only fitting, all things considered," he said coolly. A hole opened up inside her heart.

She moistened her lips. "Because of what passed between us, or because you don't wish to claim any intimate acquaintance with a divorced woman?"

"Do you think I really care about your status in society?" His tone dripped scorn.

"No. You never cared as much as I." She fingered the strings of her reticule and called herself twelve kinds of idiot for coming. She really ought to learn to say no to Aunt Millie.

He said nothing for a long moment. Then, softly, "You had more to lose." She looked up at the gentleness in his voice. Again, a tangible current passed between them.

He abruptly turned away.

Amelia swayed, unsteady by the severance of eye contact.

"Forgive me." He turned back to face her, all business now. "I failed to offer you a seat. Or refreshment."

"Nothing, thank you." Grateful to get off her wobbly legs, she sank into the nearest divan. She moistened her lips. "I suppose you're wondering why I've come. I heard you were staying here with your brother, and I needed to ask your advice. Professionally."

"Professionally?" He sat in an armchair, the table between them an effective barrier and fixed an immovable stare upon her.

"On behalf of my Aunt Millie. You see, she's

having trouble sleeping. Her current physician's remedies have become less effective than they once were."

He leaned back and carefully placed his fingers together as if matching them up. "Does she know you're here?"

"Of course. She asked me to come in her stead."

"Really? She's suddenly decided I'm worth her notice? Or has she taken pity upon an impoverished surgeon and has extended her charity to help build up my practice?"

She winced at his tone but mustered on with the same courage she'd needed when facing the board of directors. "She thought you might know of new remedies of which her old doctor is not yet aware. She said you gave something to Lady Evensley—"

"Sleep remedies are something any physician can prescribe," he interrupted. "Moreover, I don't plan to remain in London long. I'm establishing myself in the country, so you see, I don't plan to build up any sort of clientele here."

He was leaving? The thought brought on a nervous flutter akin to panic. She stammered, "A-are you? Where will you go?"

"My cousin Freddy offered me his cottage in Hampshire—you know the place." He smiled faintly.

"It's actually quite grand for a cottage; six bedrooms if you can believe it. It's mine, deed and all. Apparently there isn't a doctor or surgeon within miles. Or so he says."

She pushed through her own sorrow and tried to think of him. "Oh, Reed, I'm so glad for you. It's what you've always wanted—a practice in the country."

A wistful smile touched his mouth. "Almost everything."

She studied him, afraid to hope he might be softening toward her. His gaze moved slowly over her face as if memorizing it. Now would be a good time to say something witty or clever, but nothing came to mind.

For the briefest moments pain touched his eyes. "He actually offered it to me years ago, before I left for the war."

Back when they'd been together. Had he secured it for her?

"Reed..."

He cleared his throat. "But until I leave, tell your aunt to pay me a call and I'll be happy to give her some direction. I'll need to speak with her in person, though, so I can determine what she's already tried and if she's had any bad reactions to anything. That is, if she can bear to see me." He stood in a clear dismissal.

"She never had any objection to you, Reed. She liked you, in fact. Even my uncle approved of your character. He simply disapproved of your family and your chosen profession."

"How comforting," he said dryly.

Wishing she could think of something to say to prolong her call—ridiculous, since he clearly did not share her sentiment—she nodded, arose, and extended her hand. "Thank you."

He clasped her hand briefly but released it as if he found the contact distasteful.

She fingered the strings of her reticule. "Good day." Her footsteps echoed on the wood parquet floor as she strode to the exit. At the doorway, she turned.

His focused stare remained fixed on her. Again she cursed herself for trying too hard to please her uncle. Aunt Millie had told her if she chose against her heart, Amelia would be sorry. Aunt Millie was right. If only she'd followed her counsel! Amelia's voice cracked. "If it means anything to you, I never stopped loving you."

His body stiffened. "Good day, Mrs. Dasherwood."

His abrupt dismissal hit her with the force of a slap. She'd been stupid to think he might still care for her. She was even more stupid to continue to love a man who didn't return her feelings. Amelia left, as wounded as if she'd been well and truly trampled. Bleak loneliness opened its gaping maw and threatened to swallow her whole.

# Chapter 6

Reed spent a torturous week fighting images of Amy and the softness in her eyes as she'd said, 'I never stopped loving you.' He'd been right to turn her away, of course. Only a dolt would lay his heart at the foot of a woman twice, much less at the foot of an aristocratic woman. So if he'd been right, then why did he feel as if he'd swallowed a mace—ball, spikes and all?

He busied himself with purchasing supplies needed to open a practice in the country, as well as what he'd need to establish a home of his own. An empty home, without the touch of a woman. But there'd be other women. He would not be alone forever. He'd certainly had enough women throw themselves at him that he never doubted his looks or charm. He'd find the daughter of a country gentleman who'd be happy to marry a man of his station. He doubted he'd ever find another woman with the voice of an angel and the face of a goddess. Or with her compassion. Once, she'd found a fallen bird and had lovingly nursed it back to health, though with an injury that left it unable to fly. Did she still have that bird as a pet? No wonder she'd made a project of an orphanage. That really wasn't so unlike her at all. She'd stood her ground against his bully of a grandfather, and immediately won over the old man. Grandfather had winked at Reed and dared him to marry that girl. He'd said she had "grit." No doubt that admirable quality had carried her through a bad marriage and an ugly divorce.

Reed let out his breath in disgust. He had to purge her from his thoughts. However, six years had failed to do it, no matter how much he'd thrown himself into his work. Even the perils of living in the midst of a war had not banished memories of Amelia. He paused mid-stride as a thought occurred to him. He'd changed during their separation. No doubt, so had she. If he were to court her, he'd find that they no longer had any common interests and that a union between them would not be desirable.

Perhaps therein lay the answer. He'd court Amelia; and he'd see exactly why he didn't want her. Then he could move to the country and finally stop comparing every woman to her. He could live again. He could love again.

Best of all, the revenge would be so satisfying if

he could make her well and truly in love with him, so that when he announced he wanted nothing further to do with her, he could leave her in the same wreckage she'd left him.

Yet the thought of hurting Amy left a sting of guilt. Could he actually look her in the eye and deliberately break her heart?

The following morning, he knocked at the door of her aunt's house. Calling at this time of day broke all kinds of rules of society, instead of coming at the fashionable 'at-home' time, but perhaps he'd be forgiven due to his lowly status.

The butler looked him over as if to assess his worthiness. Then, no doubt noting the cut and fabric of his clothing, and assuming Reed to be a fashionable gentleman, asked in a respectful tone of voice, "May I help you, sir?"

Reed handed the butler his card. "Reed St. Ives to see Mrs. Dasherwood."

"Mrs. Dasherwood is not at home, sir."

Reed nodded, oddly disappointed. "Please be good enough to inform her that I have called."

"Of course, sir."

No doubt his card would be placed on a silver tray along with all the cards of other callers. Did she have many callers? The circumstances of her divorce being what they were, public opinion seemed to be that of horrified pity instead or scorn, which probably didn't make for a wide circle of friends. Most of the beau monde only accepted the publicly untainted, as he well knew. He turned away, took a hackney to a park, and ambled through the pathways. Nurses watching over children, and a few others strolled in the sun.

A horsewoman galloped down a riding path with all the regal bearing of a queen, yet pushed her mount to an almost reckless pace as if trying to outrun invisible demons chasing her. He admired her form as she neared, then sucked in his breath. The horsewoman was Amelia Dasherwood. She rode without appearing to notice him.

Yet, at the last moment, just as she passed him, her gaze flicked his way. Behind him, hoof steps slowed and then stopped.

He glanced over his shoulder. She sat turned in the saddle, motionless, with her gaze fixed upon him as if undecided whether to engage him. He'd been unforgivably cool at their last meeting. She probably needed some sign of warmth to venture an approach. He lifted his hand in a greeting and sauntered toward her with a casualness he didn't feel. He fought the inclination to run to her and bare details of his lonely existence since she walked out of his life. A man had his pride, after all.

She turned her horse around, walked toward him, and stopped a few feet away. He admired her figure as she sat side-saddle, every inch a lady, wearing a riding habit of rich purple, a tasteful and elegant bonnet perched on her head. She'd always had a flair for fashion. A few tendrils had escaped her chignon and blew around her face, giving her an earthy, approachable look.

He offered a tentative smile. "I just came from your house."

She blinked. "You did?"

"I did. I'd hoped I could entice you to go riding with me."

A faint curving of those lips came in reply. "You went to my house, without a horse, to see if I wanted to go riding with you?"

He grinned sheepishly. "I assumed you wouldn't be able to go with me on the spot, but thought I could entice you to join me tomorrow morning."

She said nothing at first, merely swept her gaze over him as if to learn all his secrets. Finally, she moistened her lips. "I accept." She smiled, yet a hint of wariness remained in her eyes.

He wanted to erase the caution in her expression

and assure her he'd never hurt her. But wasn't he planning on doing just that—woo her, discover that they didn't suit, and then leave, preferably after stealing away her heart? Shame at his own heartlessness edged through his resolve.

He cleared his throat. "I rather fancy an ice at the moment. Care to accompany me to Gunther's?" Though they were on the opposite side of the park from Gunther's, the walk would be pleasant.

"I'd be delighted." Yet that hint of caution remained.

As she made to dismount, he stepped closer to help her down. He closed his hands over her waist and lowered her to the ground, her soft body brushing against his. Gritting his teeth, he reminded himself that now was not the time to pull her into his arms.

She looked up at him, her cheeks pink from the early morning air, and her lips within easy reach. All he'd have to do is lower his head a little...

He cleared his throat and stepped back, reminding himself he needed to move slowly before he would gain her trust. Then he'd be the one walking away instead of the one left behind. After only moments in her presence, that idea began to sound less and less appealing.

As they strolled side by side, Amy led her horse

144

and cast guarded glances his way. The horse let out his breath in a whoosh and shook his head, jingling the tack. A bird sang with all its heart in a nearby tree, nearly drowning out the chorus of other birdsong.

Reed searched for a topic. "I understand you're sponsoring an orphan asylum."

Her eyes lit up. "I am. It's for this reason that I've returned to London—to gain supporters. There's so much to do."

"Have you had any luck? Finding supporters, I mean?"

"Yes, much more than I'd hoped. The Evensleys and my aunt have been of tremendous support and have recommended my venture to their friends. Some still only see me as a woman of scandal, but many have been more helpful than I expected."

"It's a worthy cause."

She smiled up at him. "Very. Oh, Reed, you should have seen them. Nearly three-fourths of the children died last year due to typhus. The survivors are so thin and weak—poor, halfstarved things without adequate heat or clothing."

Unable to stop himself, Reed said, "If I can be of any assistance, let me know. As an officer on half-pay, I haven't much to give financially, of course, but I'd be happy to offer my services as a doctor. I have studied as physician as well as a surgeon."

"That's very generous of you, thank you." Her smile turned so dazzling that Reed had to remind himself of all the reasons why he did not want to develop feelings for her.

A breeze whispered in the trees, bringing Amy's taunting perfume. He drew in a deep breath, filling his senses with her fragrance.

She spoke in a hushed voice. "Your grandfather...he doesn't support you?"

"He offers, but his gifts always come with a price. I value my independence too much."

"Of course. I meant no offence." Her mouth twisted to one side and a gleam entered her eyes. "Do you suppose he might help support an orphan asylum?"

He chuckled. "You could always ask. He is in London right now."

"I believe I shall."

They walked together, their footsteps falling synchronously. He wondered if he'd matched his pace to hers, or if she'd adjusted. They'd always found themselves walking in stride when they'd walked together in the past, her arm tucked in his, his chest swelling in pride that she was with him, of all men. How many dreams they had then!

He gave himself a mental shake. "How is your aunt? Is she still having trouble sleeping?"

"Oh, that. I suggested she pay you a call."

"I do have a rather good remedy I've developed myself and I hope to offer it to my new patients."

"I didn't realize you did that sort of thing."

He shrugged. "I've discovered an interest in the healing powers of plants as well as traditional medicine and surgery. I should have given it to you when you called. I apologize for my conduct." He inwardly winced at his abrupt dismissal.

"Think nothing of it." But hurt shone through her eyes before she lowered her lashes.

Wincing, Reed closed his eyes. Only a beast would cause her pain. He'd have to fortify himself against her if he truly meant to prove their unsuitability to himself. Otherwise, he risked losing his heart to her again.

Her voice edged into his thoughts. "How soon do you depart? For the country?"

"I'd planned to go the end of the month."

She looked up at him. Was that disappointment in her eyes? "So soon?"

"I might delay, if given the right incentive." He gave her a meaningful look. "I must admit, however, that I'm anxious to begin setting up my practice, although I suspect many my patients will include animals."

Her lips twitched. "How are you at delivering horses?"

"About as good as I am at delivering babies."

"I don't suppose you had much call for that in the middle of a war."

"You'd be surprised at how many babies I delivered, both of the four and two-legged kind. The camp followers and officers' wives produced a surprising number of them, legitimate or otherwise."

"Oh." Her face colored slightly. She glanced up at him, her lip held between her teeth, her unspoken question dangling in the air between them. Her eyes, bluer than the morning sky, began that familiar dance as if searching for answers in his.

Reed stood as if poised on the edge of a cliff. Did he have the courage to leap? "None of the babies were mine," he said softly.

She focused on the ground. "It really isn't my concern."

"Perhaps not, but I wanted you to know." His hand itched to touch her smooth cheek, and had to remind his heart not to care. His heart didn't listen.

Her breath came in audible bursts. "No one took your place in my heart." She halted and looked up at him. "I felt like an unfaithful wretch, married to him and thinking of you. Then I realized he didn't care.

He preferred it that way, even, because he was thinking of someone else, too—a different person every few days, of course—but he was never faithful to me."

"I'm sorry." And he truly was sorry, curse him for an imbecile.

"I'm sorry, too. I thought by marrying a man of whom my uncle approved, I would be assured of happiness. I was wrong." Her words came out in a rush with hurt and bitterness carved into every syllable. "I know people aren't usually surprised when married men keeping mistresses, but it hurt me to think I wasn't enough for him. At first I thought it was my fault—if I had really loved him, and had been totally faithful to him in my heart, perhaps he wouldn't have strayed." She drew in a ragged breath. "But when I found out he never gave up his mistress, and even got a new mistress every few months when he got bored of his last, and that public affair with first the opera singer and then that actress, I realized loving him would not have saved our marriage, it would only have destroyed me." She twisted the reins in trembling hands.

If only he could have protected her from all that! Reed closed his eyes. He'd been foolish to think spending more time with her would cure his obsession with her. Instead, it made it worse. Yet he was an even greater idiot for considering a future with someone whose decisions were based upon public opinion. He considered Lord

Evensley's comment that she turned him down to please her uncle more than for society's approval.

After a moment, Reed said, "If he'd been worthy of you, you would have loved him."

"I'd like to think so, but I compared every man I met to you. They always lacked in some way."

He took a steadying breath, uncertain whether her revelation left him elated, relieved, or terrified.

She let out a half sob. "The killing blow came when he began flaunting his actress, taking her to all the parties where he should have been taking me and telling everyone that she was the Fire Queen and I was the Ice Queen. The newspapers..." she choked, "had a party with that."

Reed let out his breath, shaken at her husband's cruelty. During all those years abroad, he pictured her confession how much she loved him and how she regretted turning him down, and him effectively snubbing her. He'd imagined how satisfied he'd feel to hurt her like she'd hurt him. But seeing the stark pain, the open vulnerability, only made him want to protect her. His plan to court her long enough to free

150

his heart, cracked. He curled his hands into fists, aching to peel away all the lost time between them, hold her in his arms, tuck her into his heart. Like a knight of old, he wanted to shield her from everything hurtful, vanquish her enemies, and carry her off to safety. She started walking again, and he fell into step with her.

Trees murmured in the wind, punctuated by her horse's soft clip-clop behind them. A pair of laughing children ran past with their nursemaid close on their heels. Reed watched Amy, but she kept her gaze downward, her arms folded like a shield to protect her from hurt.

He raised a hand toward her, but dropped it without touching her. "I'm amazed you ever come to London at all anymore."

"I didn't last Season. After my divorce, I stayed in the country and refused what few visitors came calling."

"What changed your mind?"

"The orphanage. I came to gain supporters for it. Aunt Millie helped me a great deal, especially these last few weeks since I've been back in Town. She's such a dear lady." Amelia glanced apologetically at him as if realizing her words might have wounded him.

Their gazes held. In her eyes swirled years of regret and sorrow. Reed had to clamp his mouth shut before he said something he'd later regret.

They passed a girl carrying a basket of violets who offered them a timid smile. She dropped her head and moved on, no doubt to the marketplace where she hoped to sell her flowers.

Amelia called to her. "I'd like a bouquet, miss."

"Oi, m'laedy, thankee kindly."

"Allow me," Reed said with a smile.

Amelia watched him guardedly as he paid the coin and then handed a bunch of flowers to her with a flourish.

"Thank you."

"My pleasure."

She lowered her head into the flowers and drew in a deep breath. Reed suspected the maneuver had more to do with avoiding his gaze more than to enjoy the scent.

Without raising her head Amelia said, "I can't believe I told you all that about my husband—former husband. You must think me a very great fool."

"I think your husband was a very great fool and I'd like to tell him so." Actually, he wanted to wring the man's neck.

Her gaze slid his way and she blinked at him. "Truly?"

152

"Certainly. And as far as your former friends, anyone who knows you is a half-wit to listen to that kind of petty rumor. You are the warmest and most caring lady I've ever known."

She halted and turned to face him fully, the full impact of her searching gaze hitting him like a sudden gust of wind. "Do you really mean that?"

"I do."

"Then...you don't hate me?"

He drew a slow breath and shook his head. "No, of course I don't hate you."

"I feared you did."

"I admit it was a bit unsettling seeing you again. I apologize for my cool greeting. And for my words in the library."

However, he could not regret the kiss.

She shook her head and began walking again. "Nothing less than I deserve, I'm sure."

"That's not true."

"I only wish I'd made better choices in the past." She glanced quickly at him. "I wish I'd had the courage to marry you when you wanted me. I know you no longer do, but it breaks my heart to think that you're leaving and I'll lose you again."

Her confession left him winded. He didn't have the armor necessary to ward off Amelia's assault. He didn't have a shield to defend himself from these weapons of honesty and longing and love.

Then she delivered the final blow. "I know you must think me shameless for declaring myself to you, but if I let you leave without telling you how I feel, I will always regret it. And believe me; I don't need any more regret. In spite of my marriage, my heart has been constant to you."

He pressed his hand to his eyes. How could he fight this? This was the Amelia he'd loved, the guileless girl who spoke her mind and loved with such innocence. But doubt clouded his thoughts if they could really be happy together, or if years of bitterness left him too closed over to give and receive love.

# Chapter 7

Shocked by her own confession, Amelia waited with her heart thudding in her ears.

Reed said nothing.

Of course he wouldn't. She was a ninny to hope he would. He no longer loved her, probably hadn't in years.

She turned away to hide her tears springing to her eyes. "Forgive me. I've made you uncomfortable. Be well, Reed. Good bye." Her voice cracked.

In an attempt to gather what little remained of her pride, she squared her shoulders and strode away without a backward glance, gripping her horse's reins as if they were the only thing keeping her upright. She used a bench as a mounting block and galloped away without looking back at Reed.

After finding a secluded area of the park, Amelia dismounted, sank down onto a bench, and sobbed. Despite the pain of saying good-bye the first time, and the ensuing years of loneliness, nothing compared to the agony of knowing what she'd lost, and would never again find. She obviously didn't deserve a second chance. She'd laid her heart at Reed's feet, and he'd failed to pick it up, or give her any hope. Perhaps it was just as well. She didn't know if she had the courage to try another relationship. Her choices before had led her to misery.

Numb and exhausted from her cry, Amelia mounted her patient horse and walked him back to Aunt Millie's Mayfair house. She left him in the care of a footman who would, no doubt, see him delivered to the mews.

"Amelia dear?" Her aunt's voice drifted from the back parlor.

"Yes, Aunt." She found Aunt Millie bent over embroidery. "Did you have a nice ride?"

Amy sank into the divan next to her aunt and kissed her cheek. "It was lovely." The muffled sounds of the street outside wormed into the room's silence and Amelia twisted her gloves in her lap.

"It's Reed St. Ives, isn't it?"

Amelia started. "I beg your pardon?"

"The reason you've been so quiet ever since Lord and Lady Evensley's party. I know it isn't because anyone said anything to you. From what I saw, they were all polite...unless someone said something in private?"

Donna Hatch

"No. The Evensley's friends were polite. I'm merely tired, Aunt. London air has never agreed with me."

"Are you certain that's all it is?"

Amelia traced the pattern of her skirt with a finger. "What do you want me to say?"

"Dearest, I know you've always tried very hard to be everything we expected of you. But there are times when one must follow one's heart, instead of living up to the ideals of others."

"I know."

"Do you really?" Aunt Millie set aside her embroidery. "I know you and Uncle loved me. You've always been very kind to me and you never made me feel a burden."

Aunt Millie, her namesake, substitute mother, and dearest friend took her hand. "You wish you'd gone against your uncle's wishes and married Reed St. Ives, don't you? Seeing him has brought it all back."

Tears stung Amelia's eyes. "Uncle was right; Reed was not a suitable match." Yet even to her, the words sounded thin and forced.

Aunt Millie let out a snort. "A love match is not such a bad thing. I told you that back in the beginning."

Amelia wiped the tears coursing down her cheeks and pushed away the images. "He wasn't suitable."

"His only flaws were his background."

"And his profession."

"I admit that was the worst of it. If he'd become a respectable physician instead of a surgeon who sullies his hands, your uncle might have been more understanding. You can't blame your uncle dear. He was trying very hard to be a good guardian for you."

"I know. I trusted him. He was usually right." Amy smiled. "Except when he disagreed with you."

Aunt Millie's mouth curved. "Yes, well, he wasn't right about Reed. Amy, dearest, you're a grown woman now, and you can make your own choices. Reed St. Ives is a good man. If you still love him, then you should make it known to him. He clearly still has strong feelings for you."

"Of the negative kind."

Aunt Millie smiled mysteriously. "Don't be too sure."

Amelia let out her breath. "I did speak with him. Against my better judgment, I told him how I feel about him but whatever he once felt for me is gone. I hurt him too badly and he no longer loves me. It's my fault."

"You were obedient to your uncle. Defying a father-figure you've spent years trying to impress is difficult when you're seventeen. Or at any age, for that matter."

Amelia pondered her aunt's words. "I should have listened to you. You tried to tell me, but I didn't listen." Amelia heaved a sigh. "It no longer matters."

Aunt Millie looked pained. "I think you should know; when Lord Forsythe asked for your hand, your uncle had doubts about him. But he couldn't bring himself to reject a lord. After you and Reed parted ways, you were so broken-hearted that your uncle couldn't bear to cause you such pain again by rejecting a second suitor. Your uncle thought if you married Lord Forsythe, you might be happy again."

Amelia nodded. "Uncle did question me regarding my feelings for Lord Forsythe, but I was reluctant to express any opinion. I relied entirely upon his judgment because I was afraid to trust mine." She let out a mirthless laugh and then shrugged. "It doesn't matter. For all I know, Reed and I would have been miserable, too."

"I doubt that." She leaned forward and touched her arm. "Amelia dear, he's come back into your life again. Don't waste this second chance."

Suddenly unable to continue this conversation, Amelia stood. "I think I'll lie down before dinner. Oh, and I've decided to return to the country Friday next."

"So soon?"

"I've had more than enough of London. I did

what I intended to do; I attended parties, faced down those who renounced me, and more importantly, secured the funds I needed for the orphanage. It's time to go home."

"Must you leave so soon? It will be so lonely without you here."

Amelia cast about for a plausible excuse. "I wish to return to oversee the improvements at the orphanage."

"I see."

The sooner she got away from London, the presence of Reed St. Ives, and all the painful memories, the better. With luck, she'd stay busy enough to push back her emptiness.

The following morning, as Amelia donned her riding gloves for her customary ride in the park, the butler announced Dr. St. Ives to see her.

Amelia's heart thumped double-time. "Very well. Show him in."

Reed entered, sweeping off his hat and extending a hand, his eyes making a slow perusal of her. His teeth flashed. "I always did love you in red."

Her breath left her in a rush. "Reed."

"You sound surprised. Did you not agree to go riding with me this morning?"

"I...I wasn't sure the offer stood."

"Have I ever broken my word?"

"No, indeed." He eyed her in that piercing way he had as if searching out all her secrets. "Do you no longer wish to accept?"

"Not at all. I ..." She glanced down at her riding habit. "I am dressed for it."

She expected him to smile but he grew grave. "If you do not wish to be in my company, tell me now and spare us both the discomfort. I'll understand if you tell me you didn't mean what you said to me yesterday."

"I do wish to go riding with you." Her words came out in a rush, and she suspected her desperation was painfully apparent. "And I meant what I said."

She winced. She'd just turned her heart inside out. She stood waiting for him to pour acid on the raw, exposed areas.

He offered her his arm. "Shall we?"

At least he hadn't rejected her. Or mocked her as he'd likely been tempted. She searched his face but found no clues as to his thoughts. They stepped outside as a stable boy appeared with her favorite bay saddled and ready for her morning ride.

Reed helped her up, his hand warm and strong on her waist, then moved away to mount a lovely chestnut gelding. They spoke of inconsequential things on the way to the park, and then rode side by side for the better part of an hour. She'd forgotten how beautifully he rode, as if he were a part of the horse instead of a separate being. They spoke little, but the silence was unexpectedly comfortable. They slowed to a walk, their horses' hooves moving in unison.

Reed glanced at her. "I never did get my ice from Gunther's. Shall we go now?"

"I'd like that." Another rider came from the opposite direction and an all-too-familiar voice rang out. "Well, well, the Ice Queen and the surgeon."

Amelia looked up and broke out into a cold sweat as she met the sneering face of her former husband, Lord Forsythe.

# Chapter 8

As the color fled from Amelia's face, Reed turned to the rider who'd spoken. Cold anger settled into his stomach. He inclined his head but did not bother to keep the malice out of his voice. "Lord Forsythe."

Amelia's former husband barely spared him a glance. "You look positively ill, my dear. Perhaps it's that color. I never did like you in red. Or maybe unmarried life does not suit you after all?"

"You do not suit me," Amelia shot back.

"No, we never were a good pair. But at least I got your dowry for my trouble, so I suppose it wasn't a complete waste."

Reed's cold anger turned into a hot rage. "Watch yourself, sir, lest I take exception to your behavior toward the lady."

Lord Forsythe laughed, sharp and mirthless. "You do play the lover well, St. Ives, but I know better. And really, she isn't worth the trouble."

"She's worth far more than a cowardly snake like you is capable of giving."

Lord Forsythe's eyes narrowed. "I suppose you think because you survived a war that you're brave. But do not make the mistake of crossing me."

Reed maneuvered his horse closer to the lord and stared him down. "Do not make the mistake of insulting Amy either in public or private again or I assure you, I will ensure that you will regret it."

Lord Forsythe scoffed, but a hesitant light touched his eye. "You do not intimidate me."

"Leave. Her. Be."

Amelia's former husband sneered but uneasiness touched his posture. "I told you; she isn't worth it." He looked Amelia over from head to toe. "Farewell, Ice Queen. Maybe this hotblooded fool will warm your frigid heart. I care not."

Amy raised her chin. "I wish you well, Lord Forsythe. I'm sure some day you'll find a woman who loves you in spite of all your flaws. I truly hope you don't simply die of some horrible disease you picked up at a brothel."

With a murderous glint in his eyes Lord Forsythe moved closer. Reed leaped forward to intervene, but didn't need to; Amy brought up her riding crop, poised to strike.

Lord Forsythe let out a scoff. "You aren't worth the trouble." He spurred his horse and left them.

Reed took a calming breath, still wishing he could have strangled the heartless cad.

Amelia's ragged breathing drew his attention. She pressed her lips into a tight line, and her hands clenched her reins as if trying to squeeze the life out of them.

"Amy." He moved his horse next to hers, close enough that his leg brushed against her mare. He reached out and took her trembling hands in his. "He can't hurt you anymore."

She gripped his hand as if she depended upon it to remain upright. "I don't know why I let him upset me so." She let out a half sob. "To think I once thought I might someday love him."

"He puts on a charming veneer when he chooses to."

"I won't make that mistake a second time."

"What? Falling for the charms of a rake, or getting married?"

"Trying to please someone else instead of listening to my heart." She drew in a breath and squared her shoulders. "Thank you for the ride."

Reed roused himself. "I'll escort you back."

They rode in silence, Amelia looking straight ahead as if unaware of his presence. They left their horses in the care of a pair of stable lads, one who mounted Amelia's and rode it back to the mews, the other held the reins of Reed's horse.

Reed walked her up the stairs to the front door. Inside the foyer, they stood awkwardly, Reed searching for a safe topic, wishing for what might have been, or what could be...

Amy offered her hand. "Thank you for the ride. It was lovely to see you again. Good luck in the country. I, too, am returning home on Friday."

The wind left his lungs. "Friday?" he wheezed.

"My work here is complete. It's time. Good bye, Reed." She turned and disappeared into a nearby room, softly closing the door behind her.

Stunned, Reed stood with his hat in his hands. Friday. He'd never see her again. A wide, gaping hole tore open inside him.

A voice broke through his thoughts. "If you still care for her, you'd best make yourself known." Amy's Aunt Millie stood watching him.

Reed stammered, "She and I ...we...I'm not sure we suit."

She smiled wisely. "Is that your whole heart speaking, or just the wounded part?"

He opened his mouth but could make no reply. "She rejected you to please her uncle. Not because she didn't love you. She loves you still."

Reed took a breath. Then another.

She nodded as a triumphant gleam entered her eye. "Good day, Dr. St. Ives."

He rasped out, "Good day, madam." He left, more uncertain of his course than ever. He'd hoped by spending time with Amelia, he could prove to himself that she no longer meant anything to him. But after only a few short hours, he suspected if he let Amelia walk out of his life again, he'd never survive the loss.

# Chapter 9

Amelia's normal excitement before a trip remained notably absent. Instead of the usual anticipation, only a dull sorrow remained her companion as she stood in the foyer of Aunt Millie's London house and surveyed the servants carrying out her trunks.

In the midst of it, a visitor arrived. "Reed St. Ives to see you, madam."

Amelia closed her eyes, wishing she could close her heart.

"Amy." Reed came to her, his dear face as welcome as a rain shower in a drought.

She shielded herself against his allure. Against her own heart. "I'm afraid this isn't a good time. I'm about to return home."

"I know. That's why I'm here. Please walk with me."

She hesitated, torn between her heart and her head. "I'm due to leave within the hour."

He grinned a bit lopsidedly and gestured toward

the private coach waiting in the street in front of the door. "I really don't think they'll leave without you."

She couldn't help but smile. "No, I suppose not." She donned her pelisse and took his offered arm.

"Shall we go to the walking park?"

"If you wish." The walking park. How many times had they walked there together before? She hadn't been in years; it held too many memories of Reed.

He guided them down the path between houses to the park behind. The noises of the city faded away in that quiet harbor of green. Automatically, they headed to the duck pond. Two white swans glided by in graceful splendor on the glass-like surface.

Amelia tried to read his expression, but he'd gotten much better at disguising his thoughts. "I hope I didn't shock you the other day when I poured out all the ugly details of my marriage. You probably felt somewhat vindicated learning how unsuitable I really am with such an unsavory past."

He stopped walking and turned to her, his jaw clenched. "Give me a little, credit, Amy. Do you really think me so petty?"

She dropped her head. "I never thought you petty."

"Then you can't think I'd judge you based on the way a cad treated you."

169

"Others do."

"And I'm like them?"

She looked up at him but couldn't meet his accusing eyes. "You're nothing like them. But so many people have turned out to be different than they seemed that I hardly know whom to trust."

His voice quieted. "That's understandable considering what you've endured."

She looked away. The tree where he'd carved a heart met her eyes. She moved her gaze to the stone bench but could only see the place where he'd first kissed her.

Suddenly claustrophobic with memories and the crushing fear about to overwhelm her, she burst out, "Reed, I must apologize. I spoke out of turn. I can see now that you and I are not meant for one another and I was wrong to speak of emotions of which I know nothing, and of which you clearly do not return."

His gaze hardened. "Then you truly feel nothing for me."

"Yes. No! I do love you but I..." She let out a low moan, turned and began walking away.

"Amy."

She quickened her pace and called over her shoulder, "Please don't." She all but ran away from him.

170

"Amy, wait!" Heavy footsteps pounded after her. He gripped her elbow and tugged until she turned to face him. Excitement mingled with uncertainty in his eyes. His hand slid down her arm to her hand. "No matter how hard I tried, my feelings for you have not changed."

She eyed him, searching for signs of mockery but only found intensity. Then he smiled, that same slow, tender smile he used to give her that always made her pulse leap. It had the same effect now. Hope glimmered in her heart.

He continued, "But everything about me that your uncle found unsuitable remains the same. My grandfather is the owner of a mill."

"I know."

"And my parents are social climbers."

"Apparently so."

"And I'm a doctor. Not just a physician—a surgeon. My hands are tainted by trade."

"I don't care about any of that now any more than I did six years ago. I only refused you because my uncle didn't approve, and I just couldn't...I was afraid..."

"I know." He smiled with such tenderness that a lump formed in her throat. "Last week when I went to your house, it was with the intent to court you long enough to prove that we don't suit, social reasons aside."

. "I see." She looked down and took a step away.

He tightened his grip on her hand, halting her footsteps. "That was a foolish intent."

She again searched his face for signs of deceit, warning her heart not to hope. Her heart refused to listen. "How foolish?"

"I love you, Amy. I never stopped loving you. I love you more now because I know how empty I am without you."

She swallowed hard, her eyes stinging with unshed tears. "You do?"

He placed a gentle hand on her cheek. "I promise you, if you'll have me, I will spend my every breath making you happy."

She went still.

"Come with me to the country, and be a country doctor's wife. Marry me."

She let out a little sob and tightened her grip on his hand. Now that the moment was here, she was suddenly afraid. "I'm divorced—a woman of scandal."

"I'm a doctor—unfit for the daughter of a lord."

"In my four years of marriage, I failed to conceive."

"You're not a broodmare, Amy. I'll love you whether or not we have babies."

She stared. "But you love children."

"As do you. We may yet have them. Sometimes it's the man, not the woman, who can't procreate." He enfolded her hands inside his.

She nodded doubtfully, still fearing this was somehow a dream. If so, she never wanted to awaken.

"If not," he added, "we can always take in some poor waif who needs a family."

She let out a half sob, half laugh. "I'm certain there's no shortage of those. I happen to know of a whole orphanage full of children who need to be loved." She searched his eyes. "What about the orphanage? I can't abandon it now."

"Of course you won't. We'll travel there together as often as you think we ought. You mentioned it had a new director?"

"Yes, a couple."

"Are they competent?" he asked.

"Oh, yes, and very dedicated."

"Will they treat the children well?"

She nodded. "Yes, they both have demonstrated kindness and compassion, and the children already seem quite devoted to them."

"Then let them do their work, and we'll visit as often as you see the need."

Still hardly daring to believe this was happening,

she nodded. "It would only be a day's journey from your cottage."

"Our cottage, if you'll have it. And me." Reed softly caressed her cheek. "Do you still love me, Amy?"

She let out her breath. "You know I do."

"I need to hear it again." He gave her that familiar playful grin that never failed to melt her heart.

She drew a shaking breath. Reed was not a rake. Violence and infidelity were not in his nature. He was a man of honor who listened to his conscience and possessed a strong sense of honor. And he was uncommonly gentle. Amelia had never seen him angry except when her former husband had bullied her in the park.

"I love you, Reed St. Ives."

Joy leaped into his eyes. "I love you, too...er, what was your name, again?"

She laughed and swatted his arm. Chuckling, he pulled her into an embrace. She nestled into the protective shelter of his arms and laid her cheek against his chest.

Reed rested his chin on the top of her head. "Marry me, Amy."

She nodded, never more sure of anything in her life. He was a good man who would love and cherish her. Her heart had not chosen unwisely.

"Of course I will."

He dipped his head down for a kiss. If she thought the last time they kissed had shaken her, this one threatened to knock her off her feet. The sound and light of the world around them faded away and there was only Reed, his warm mouth, his clean, earthy scent, his strong body. Along with racing desire, peace and contentment filled her.

Amelia was home.

When their lips parted, he brushed her hair back from her face. She'd feared such a moment would leave her terrified. Instead, his love healed her. They stood smiling at each other, first with hesitation, then with growing warmth, and the armor around her heart fell away. He placed a hand on her cheek, caressing with his thumb. "What will your aunt think?"

She smiled. "She told me the same thing last night that she told me years ago; she advised me to run off to Gretna Green with you."

He blinked, then a slow grin overcame his face. "What a sensible woman. I always liked her. Besides, she thinks my sleeping herbs are genius."

"I'm already packed, you know. Shall we take the coach to Gretna Green instead?"

A dark brow lifted. "An excellent idea. I can be ready to depart in ten minutes."

She laughed. "No need to hurry. There won't be any disgruntled family members chasing us to stop the marriage."

"No, but I have another reason to be in a hurry to marry you; I fear I cannot wait much longer." With a wolfish grin, he hauled her into his arms and proceeded to show her just how badly he wanted to rush the wedding.

When their lips parted, he took her hand and strode so swiftly back toward Aunt Millie's house that she had to trot to keep up. Hot and flushed from his kiss, she laughed and fanned herself with a hand. Amelia blushed as she realized they'd kissed in public. But she honestly couldn't find it in her to care.

"I think I need that ice from Gunther's you promised me."

"Anything for you, beloved. You can eat it in the carriage on the way to Scotland. I might need to pour several over my head." His eyes glittered as he draped an arm around her shoulders and escorted her into their new life together.

The End.

For other books by this author, or for more information and to take place in contests, giveaways, and behind-the-scenes sneak peeks:

Website: www.donnahatch.com
Blog: www.donnahatch.com/blog

Connect on Facebook:
www.facebook.com/RomanceAuthorDonnaHatch/
Follow on Twitter: twitter.com/donnahatch

If you like this book, please help spread the word and rate it on Amazon, Goodreads, and other book review sites.

Thank you!

# About the author:

Donna Hatch, author of the best-selling "Rogue Hearts Series," is a hopeless romantic and adventurer at heart, the force behind driving her to write and publish 13 historical titles, to date. She is a multi-award winner, a sought-after workshop presenter, and juggles multiple volunteer positions as well as her six children. Also music lover, she sings and plays the harp. Though a native of Arizona, she and her family recently transplanted to the Pacific Northwest where she and her husband of over twenty years are living proof that there really is a happily ever after.

Made in the USA
Columbia, SC
03 August 2020